# THE ISLINGTON MYSTERY

# MYSTERY

# and other stories

by

ARTHUR MACHEN

ISBN 978-1-78139-032-0

# Contents

# THE ISLINGTON MYSTERY

# I

The public taste in murders is often erratic, and sometimes, I think, fallible enough. Take, for example, that Crippen business. It happened seventeen years ago, and it is still freshly remembered and discussed with interest. Yet it was by no means a murder of the first rank. What was there in it? The outline is crude enough; simple, easy, and disgusting, as Dr. Johnson observed of another work of art. Crippen was cursed with a nagging wife of unpleasant habits; and he cherished a passion for his typist. Whereupon he poisoned Mrs. Crippen, cut her up and buried the pieces in the coal-cellar. This was well enough, though elementary; and if the foolish little man had been content to lie quiet and do nothing, he might have lived and died peaceably. But he must need to disappear from his house—the action of a fool—and cross the Atlantic with his typist absurdly and obviously disguised as a boy: sheer, bungling imbecility. Here, surely, there is no single trace of the master's hand; and yet, as I say, the Crippen Murder is reckoned amongst the masterpieces. It is the same tale in all the arts: the low comedian was always sure of a laugh if he cared to tumble over a pin; and the weakest murderer is sure of a certain amount of respectful attention if he will take the trouble to dismember his subject. And then, with respect to Crippen: he was caught by means of the wireless device, then in its early stages. This, of course, was utterly irrelevant to the true issue; but the public wallows in irrelevance. A great art critic may praise a great picture, and make his criticism a masterpiece in itself. He will be un-read; but let some asinine paragraphist say that the painter always sings "Tom Bowling" as he sets his palette, and dines on boiled fowl and apricot sauce three times a week—then the world will proclaim the artist great.

# II

The success of the second-rate is deplorable in itself; but it is more deplorable in that it very often obscures the genuine master-piece. If the crowd runs after the false, it must neglect the true. The intolerable Romola is praised; the admirable Cloister and the Hearth is waived aside. So, while the very indifferent and clumsy perform-ance of Crippen filled the papers, the extraordinary Battersea Murder was served with a scanty paragraph or two in obscure cor-ners of the Press. Indeed, we were so shamefully starved of detail that I only retain a bare outline of this superb crime in my memory; but, roughly, the affair was shaped as follows: In the first floor of one of the smaller sets of flats in Battersea a young fellow (? 18—20) was talking to an actress, a "touring" actress of no particular fame, whose age, if I recollect, was drawing on from thirty to forty. A shot, a near shot, broke in suddenly on their talk. The young man dashed out of the flat, down the stairs, and there, in the entry of the flats, found his own father, shot dead. The father, it should be remarked, was a touring actor, and an old friend of the lady upstairs. But here comes the magistral element in this murder. Beside the dead man, or in the hand of the dead man, or in a pocket of the dead man's coat—I am not sure how it was—there was found a weapon made of heavy wire—a vile and most deadly contraption, fashioned with curious and malignant ingenuity. It was night-time, but the bright light of a moon ten days old was shining, and the young man said he saw someone running and leaping over walls.

But mark the point: the dead actor was hiding beneath his friend's flat, hiding and lying in wait, with his villainous weapon to his hand. He was expecting an encounter with some enemy, on whom he was resolved to work at least deadly mischief, if not murder.

Who was that enemy? Whose bullet was it that was swifter than the dead man's savage and premeditated desire?

We shall probably never know. A murder that might have stood in the very first rank, that might have vied with the affair of Madeleine Smith—there were certain indications that made this seem possible—was suffered to fade into obscurity, while the foolish crowd surged about elementary Crippen and his bungling imbecilities. So there were once people who considered Robert Elsmere as a literary work of palmary significance.

# III

Naturally, and with some excuse, the war was responsible for a good deal of this sort of neglect. In those appalling years there was but one thing in men's heads; all else was blotted out. So, little attention was paid to the affair of the woman's body, carefully wrapped in sacking, which was found in Regent's Square, by the Gray's Inn Road. A man was hanged without phrases, but there were one or two curious points in the case.

Then, again, there was the Wimbledon Murder, a singular business. A well-to-do family had just moved into a big house facing the Common, so recently that many of its goods and chattels were still in the packing-cases. The master of the house was murdered one night by a man who made off with his booty. It was a curious haul, consisting of a mackintosh worth, perhaps, a couple of pounds, and a watch which would have been dear at ten shillings. This murderer, too, was hanged without comment; and yet, on the face of it, his conduct seems in need of explanation. But the most singular case of all those that suffered from the preoccupations of the war was, there is no doubt, the Islington Mystery, as the Press called it. It was a striking headline, but the world was too busy to attend. The affair got abroad, so far as it did get abroad, about the time of the first employment of the tanks; and people were trying not to see through the war correspondents, not to perceive that the inky fandangoes and corroborees of these gentlemen hid a sense of failure and disappointment.

# IV

But as to the Islington Mystery—this is how it fell out. There is an odd street, not far from the region which was once called Spa Fields, not far from the Pentonville or Islington Fields, where Grimaldi the clown was once accused of inciting the mob to chase an overdriven ox. It goes up a steep hill, and the rare adventurer who pierces now and then into this unknown quarter of London is amazed and bewildered at the very outset, since there are no steep hills in the London of his knowledge, and the contours of the scene remind him of the cheap lodging-house area at the back of hilly seaside resorts. But if the site is strange, the buildings on it are far stranger. They were no doubt set up at the high tide of Sir Walter Scott Gothic, which has left such queer memorials behind it. The houses of Lloyd Street are in couples, and the architect, combining the two into one design, desired to create an illusion of a succession of churches, in the Perpendicular or Third Pointed manner, climbing up the hill. The detail is rich, there are finials to rejoice the heart, and gargoyles of fine fantasy, all carried out in the purest stucco. At the lowest house on the right-hand side lived Mr. Harold Boale and his wife, and a brass plate on the Gothic door said, "Taxidermist: Skeletons Articulated". As it chanced, this lowest house of Lloyd Street has a longer garden than its fellows, giving on a contractor's yard, and at the end of the garden Mr. Boale had set up the apparatus of his craft in an outhouse, away from the noses of his fellow-men.

So far as can be gathered, the stuffer and articulator was a harmless and inoffensive little fellow. His neighbours liked him, and he and the Boule cabinet-maker from next door, the Shell box-maker over the way, the seal-engraver and the armourer from Baker Square at the top of the hill, and the old mercantile marine skipper who lived round the corner in Marchmont Street, at the house with the ivory junk in the window, used to spend many a genial evening together in the parlour of the Quill in the days before everything was spoilt by the war.

They did not drink very much or talk very much, any of them; but they enjoyed their moderate cups and the snug comfort of the place, and stared solemnly at the old coaching prints that were upon the walls, and at the large glass painting depicting the landing of England's Injured Queen, which hung over the mantelpiece, between two Pink Dogs with gold collars. Mr. Boale passed as a very nice sort of man in this circle and everybody was sorry for him. Mrs. Boale was a tartar and a scold. The men of the quarter kept out of her way; the women were afraid of her. She led poor Boale the devil's own life. Her voice, often enough, would be heard at the Quill door, vomiting venom at her husband's address; and he, poor man, would tremble and go forth, lest some worse thing might happen. Mrs. Boale was a short dark woman. Her hair was coal-black, her face wore an expression of acid malignity, and she walked quickly but with a decided limp. She was full of energy and the pest of the neighbourhood, and more than a pest to her husband.

The war, with its scarcity and its severe closing-hours, made the meetings at the Quill rarer than before, and deprived them of a good deal of their old comfort. Still, the circle was not wholly broken up, and one evening Boale announced that his wife had gone to visit relations in Lancashire, and would most likely be away for a considerable time.

"Well, there's nothing like a change of air, so they say," said the skipper, "though I've had more than enough of it myself."

The others said nothing, but congratulated Boale in their hearts. One of them remarked afterwards that the only change that would do Mrs. Boale good was a change to Kingdom Come, and they all agreed. They were not aware that Mrs. Boale was enjoying the advantages of the recommended treatment.

# V

As I recollect, Mr. Boale's worries began with the appearance of Mrs. Boale's sister, Mary Aspinall, a woman almost as ill-tempered and malignant as Mrs. Boale herself. She had been for some years nurse with a family in Capetown, and had come home with her mistress. In the first place, the woman had written two or three letters to her sister, and there had been no reply. This struck her as odd, for Mrs. Boale had been a very good correspondent, filling her letters with "nasty things" about her husband. So, on her first afternoon off after her return, Mary Aspinall called at the house in Lloyd Street to get the truth of the matter from her sister's own lips. She strongly suspected Boale of having suppressed her letters. "The dirty little tyke; I'll serve him," she said to herself. So came Miss Aspinall to Lloyd Street and brought out Boale from his workshop. And when he saw her his heart sank. He had read her letters. But the decision to return to England had been taken suddenly; Miss Aspinall had, therefore, said not a word about it. Boale had thought of his wife's sister as established at the other end of the world for the next ten, twenty years, perhaps; and he meant to go away and lose himself under a new name in a year or two. And so, when he saw the woman, his heart sank.

Mary Aspinall went straight to the point.

"Where's Elizabeth?" she asked. "Upstairs? I wonder she didn't come down when she heard the bell."

"No," said Boale. He comforted himself with the thought

of the curious labyrinth he had drawn about his secret; he felt secure in the centre of it.

"No, she's not upstairs. She's not in the house."

"Oh, indeed. Not in the house. Gone to see some friends, I suppose. When do you expect her back?"

"The truth is, Mary, that I don't expect her back. She's left me—three months ago, it is."

"You mean to tell me that! Left you! Showed her sense, I think. Where has she gone?"

"Upon my word, Mary, I don't know. We had a bit of a to-do one evening, though I don't think I said much. But she said she'd had enough, and she packed a few things in a bag, and off she went. I ran after her and called to her to come back, but she wouldn't so much as turn her head, and went off King's Cross way. And from that day to this I've never seen her, nor had a word from her. I've had to send all her letters back to the post office."

Mary Aspinall stared hard at her brother-in-law and pondered. Beyond telling him that he had brought it on himself, there seemed nothing to say. So she dealt with Boale on those lines very thoroughly, and made an indignant exit from the parlour. He went back to stuff peacocks, for all I know. He was feeling comfortable again. There had been a very unpleasant sensation in the stomach for a few seconds—a very horrible fear at the moment that one of the outer walls of that labyrinth of his had been breached; but now all was well again.

And all might have been permanently well if Miss Aspinall had not happened to meet Mrs. Horridge in the main road, close to the bottom of Lloyd Street. Mrs. Horridge was the wife of the Shell box-maker, and the two had met once or twice long ago at Mrs. Boale's tea-table. They recognized each other, and, after a few unmeaning remarks, Mrs. Horridge asked Miss Aspinall if she had seen her sister since her return to England.

"How could I see her when I don't know where she is?"

asked Miss Aspinall with some ferocity.

"Dear me, you haven't seen Mr. Boale, then?"

"I've just come from him this minute."

"But he can't have lost the Lancashire address, surely?"

And so one thing led to another, and Mary Aspinall gathered quite clearly that Boale had told his friends that his wife was paying a long visit to relations in Lancashire. In the first place the Aspinalls had no relations in Lancashire—they came from Suffolk—and secondly Boale had informed her that Elizabeth had gone away in a rage, he knew not where. She did not pay him another visit then and there, as she had at first intended. It was growing late, and she took her considerations back with her to Wimbledon, determined on thinking the matter out.

Next week she called again at Lloyd Street. She charged Boale with deliberate lying, placing frankly before him the two tales he had told. Again that horrid sinking sensation lay heavy upon Boale. But he had reserves.

"Indeed," he said, "I've told you no lies, Mary. It all happened just as I said before. But I did make up that tale about Lancashire for the people about here. I didn't like them to have my troubles to talk over, especially as Elizabeth is bound to come back some time, and I hope it will be soon."

Miss Aspinall stared at the little man in a doubtful, threatening fashion for a moment, and then hurried upstairs. She came down soon afterwards.

"I've gone through Elizabeth's drawers," she said with defiance. "There's a good many things missing. I don't see those bits of lace she had from Granny, and the set of jet is gone, and so is the garnet necklace, and the coral brooch. I couldn't find the ivory fan, either."

"I found all the drawers wide open after she'd gone," sighed Mr. Boale. "I supposed she'd taken the things away with her."

It must be confessed that Mr. Boale, taught, perhaps, by

the nicety of his craft, had paid every attention to detail. He had realized that it would be vain to tell a tale of his wife going away and leaving her treasures behind her. And so the treasures had disappeared.

Really, the Aspinall vixen did not know what to say. She had to confess that Boale had explained the difficulty of his two stories quite plausibly. So she informed him that he was more like a worm than a man, and banged the hall door. Again Boale went back to his workshop with a warmth about his heart. His labyrinth was still secure, its secret safe. At first, when confronted again by the accusing Aspinall, he had thought of bolting the moment he got the woman out of the house; but that was unreasoning panic. He was in no danger. And he remembered, like the rest of us, the Crippen case. It was running away that had brought Crippen to ruin; if he had sat tight he would have sat secure, and the secret of the cellar would never have been known. Though, as Mr. Boale reflected, anybody was welcome to search his cellar, to search here and there and anywhere on his premises, from the hall door in front to the workshop at the back. And he proceeded to give his calm, whole-souled attention to a fine raven that had been sent round in the morning.

Miss Aspinall took the extraordinary disappearance of her sister back with her to Wimbledon and thought it over. She thought it over again and again, and she could make nothing of it. She did not know that people are constantly disappearing for all sorts of reasons; that nobody hears anything about such cases unless some enterprising paper sees matter for a "stunt", and rouses all England to hunt for John Jones or Mrs. Carraway. To Miss Aspinall, the vanishing of Elizabeth Boale seemed a portent and a wonder, a unique and terrible event; and she puzzled her head over it, and still could find no exit from her labyrinth—a different structure from the labyrinth maintained by the serene Boale. The Aspinall had no suspicions of her brother-in-law; both his

11

manner and his matter were straightforward, clear, and square. He was a worm, as she had informed him, but he was certainly telling the truth. But the woman was fond of her sister, and wanted to know where she had gone and what had happened to her; and so she put the matter into the hands of the police.

# VI

She furnished the best description that she could of the missing woman, but the officer in charge of the case pointed out that she had not seen her sister for many years, and that Mrs Boale was obviously the person to be consulted in the matter. So the taxidermist was again drawn from his scientific labours. He was shown the information laid by Miss Aspinall and the description furnished by her. He told his simple story once more, mentioning the incident of his lying to his neighbours to avoid unpleasant gossip, and added several details to Miss Aspinall's picture of his wife. He then furnished the constable with two photographs, pointed out the better likeness of the two, and saw his visitor off the premises with cheerful calm.

In due course, the "Missing" bill, garnished with a reproduction of the photograph selected by Mr. Boale, with minute descriptive details, including the "marked limp", was posted up at the police-stations all over the country, and glanced at casually by a few passers-by here and there. There was nothing sensational about the placard; and the statement "Last seen going in the direction of King's Cross" was not a very promising clue for the amateur detective. No hint of the matter got into the Press; as I have pointed out, hardly one per cent of these cases of "missing" does get into the Press. And just then we were all occupied in reading the pæans of the war correspondents, who were proving that an advance of a mile and a half on a nine-mile front constituted a victory which threw Waterloo into the shade. There was no room for discussing the whereabouts of an obscure woman whom Islington knew no more.

It was sheer accident that brought about the catastrophe. James Curry, a medical student who had rooms in Percy Street, Tottenham Court Road, was prowling about his quarter one afternoon in an indefinite and idle manner, gazing at shop windows and mooning at street corners. He knew that he would never want a cash register, but he inspected the stock with the closest attention, and chose a fine specimen listed at £75. Again, he invested heavily in costly Oriental rugs, and furnished a town mansion in the Sheraton manner at very considerable expense. And so his tour of inspection brought him to the police-station; and there he proceeded to read the bills posted outside, including the bill relating to Elizabeth Boale.

"Walks with a marked limp."

James Curry felt his breath go out of his body in a swift gasp. He put out a hand towards the railing to steady himself as he read that amazing sentence over again. And then he walked straight into the police-station.

The fact was that he had bought from Harold Boale, three weeks after the date on which Elizabeth Boale was last seen, a female skeleton. He had got it comparatively cheaply because of the malformation of one of the thigh-bones. And now it struck him that the late owner of that thigh-bone must have walked with a very marked limp.

# VII

M'Aulay made his reputation at the trial. He defended Harold Boale with magnificent audacity. I was in court—it was a considerable part of my business in those days to frequent the Old

Bailey—and I shall never forget the opening phrases of his speech for the prisoner. He rose slowly, and let his glance go slowly round the court. His eyes rested at last with grave solemnity on the jury. At length he spoke, in a low, clear, deliberate voice, weighing, as it seemed, every word he uttered.

"Gentlemen," he began, "a very great man, and a very wise man, and a very good man once said that probability is the guide of life. I think you will agree with me that this is a weighty utterance. When we once leave the domain of pure mathematics, there is very little that is certain. Supposing we have money to invest: we weigh the pros and cons of this scheme and that, and decide at last on probable grounds. Or it may be our lot to have to make an appointment; we have to choose a man to fill a responsible position in which both honesty and sagacity are of the first consequence. Again probability must guide us to a decision. No one man can form a certain and infallible judgment of another. And so through all the affairs of life: we must be content with probability, and again and again with probability. Bishop Butler was right.

"But every rule has its exception. The rule which we have just laid down has its exception. That exception confronts you terribly, tremendously, at this very moment. You may think—I do not say that you do think—but you may think that Harold Boale, the prisoner at the bar, in all probability murdered his wife, Elizabeth Boale."

There was a long pause at this point. Then:

"If you think that, then it is your imperative duty to acquit the prisoner at the bar. The only verdict which you dare give is a verdict of 'Not Guilty'."

Up to this, moment, Counsel had maintained the low, deliberate utterance with which he had begun his speech, pausing now and again and seeming to consider within himself the precise value of every word that came to his lips. Suddenly his voice rang out, resonant, piercing. One word followed swiftly on another:

"This, remember, is not a court of probability. Bishop Butler's maxim does not apply here. Here there is no place for probability. This is a court of certainty. And unless you are certain that my client is guilty, unless you are as certain of his guilt as you are certain that two and two make four, then you must acquit him.

"Again, and yet again—this is a court of certainty. In the ordinary affairs of life, as we have seen, we are guided by probability. We sometimes makes mistakes; in most cases these mistakes may be rectified. A disastrous investment may be counterbalanced by a prosperous investment; a bad servant may be replaced by a good one. But in this place, where life and death hang in the balances which are in your hands, there is no room for mistakes, since here mistakes are irreparable. You cannot bring a dead man back to life. You must not say, 'This man is probably a murderer, and therefore he is guilty.' Before you bring in such a verdict, you must be able to say, 'This man is certainly a murderer.' And that you cannot say, and I will tell you why."

M'Aulay then took the evidence piece by piece. Scientific witnesses had declared that the malformation of the thighbone in the skeleton exhibited would produce exactly the sort of limp which had characterized Elizabeth Boale. Counsel for the defense had worried the doctors, had made them admit that such a malformation was by no means unique. It was uncommon. Yes, but not very uncommon? Perhaps not.

Finally, one doctor admitted that in the course of thirty years of hospital and private practice he had known of five such cases of malformation of the thigh-bone. M'Aulay gave an inaudible sigh of relief; he felt that he had got his verdict.

He made all this quite clear to the jury. He dwelt on the principle that no one can be condemned unless the corpus delicti, the body, or some identifiable portion of the body of the murdered person can be produced. He told them the story of the Campden Wonder; how the "murdered" man walked into his village two years after three people had been hanged for murdering him. "Gentlemen," he said, "for all I know, and for all you know, Elizabeth Boale may walk into this court at any moment. I say boldly that we have no earthly right to assume that she is dead."

Of course Boale's defence was a very simple one. The skeleton which he sold to Mr. Curry had been gradually assembled by him in the course of the last three years. He pointed out that the two hands were not a very good match; and, indeed, this was a little detail that he had not overlooked.

The jury took half an hour to consider their verdict. Harold Boale was found "Not Guilty".

He was seen by an old friend a couple of years ago. He had emigrated to America, and was doing prosperously in his old craft in a big town of the Middle West. He had married a pleasant girl of Swedish extraction.

"You see," he explained, "the lawyers told me I should be safe in presuming poor Elizabeth's death."

He smiled amiably.

And finally, I beg to state that this account of mine is a grossly partial narrative. For all I know, assuming for a moment the severe standards of M'Aulay, Boale was an innocent man. It is possible that his story was a true one. Elizabeth Boale may, after all, be living; she may return after the fashion of the "murdered" man in the Campden Wonder. All the thoughts, devices, meditations that I have put into the heart and mind of Boale may be my own malignant inventions without the shadow of true substance behind them.

In theory, then, the Islington Mystery is an open question. Certainly; but in fact?

THE END

# A FRAGMENT
# OF LIFE

# I

Edward Darnell awoke from a dream of an ancient wood, and of a clear well rising into grey film and vapour beneath a misty, glimmering heat; and as his eyes opened he saw the sunlight bright in the room, sparkling on the varnish of the new furniture. He turned and found his wife's place vacant, and with some confusion and wonder of the dream still lingering in his mind, he rose also, and began hurriedly to set about his dressing, for he had overslept a little, and the 'bus passed the corner at 9.15. He was a tall, thin man, dark-haired and dark-eyed, and in spite of the routine of the City, the counting of coupons, and all the mechanical drudgery that had lasted for ten years, there still remained about him the curious hint of a wild grace, as if he had been born a creature of the antique wood, and had seen the fountain rising from the green moss and the grey rocks.

The breakfast was laid in the room on the ground floor, the back room with the French windows looking on the garden, and before he sat down to his fried bacon he kissed his wife seriously and dutifully. She had brown hair and brown eyes, and though her lovely face was grave and quiet, one would have said that she might have awaited her husband under the old trees, and bathed in the pool hollowed out of the rocks.

They had a good deal to talk over while the coffee was poured out and the bacon eaten, and Darnell's egg brought in by the stupid, staring servant-girl of the dusty face. They had been married for a year, and they had got on excellently, rarely sitting silent for more than an hour, but for the past few weeks Aunt Marian's present had afforded a subject for conversation which seemed inexhaustible. Mrs. Darnell had been Miss Mary Reynolds, the daughter of an auctioneer and estate agent in Notting Hill, and Aunt Marian was her mother's sister, who was supposed rather to have lowered herself by marrying a coal merchant, in a small way, at Turnham Green.

Marian had felt the family attitude a good deal, and the Reynoldses were sorry for many things that had been said, when the coal merchant saved money and took up land on building leases in the neighbourhood of Crouch End, greatly to his advantage, as it appeared. Nobody had thought that Nixon could ever do very much; but he and his wife had been living for years in a beautiful house at Barnet, with bow-windows, shrubs, and a paddock, and the two families saw but little of each other, for Mr. Reynolds was not very prosperous. Of course, Aunt Marian and her husband had been asked to Mary's wedding, but they had sent excuses with a nice little set of silver apostle spoons, and it was feared that nothing more was to be looked for. However, on Mary's birthday her aunt had written a most affectionate letter, enclosing a cheque for a hundred pounds from 'Robert' and herself, and ever since the receipt of the money the Darnells had discussed the question of its judicious disposal. Mrs. Darnell had wished to invest the whole sum in Government securities, but Mr. Darnell had pointed out that the rate of interest was absurdly low, and after a good deal of talk he had persuaded his wife to put ninety pounds of the money in a safe mine, which was paying five per cent. This was very well, but the remaining ten pounds, which Mrs. Darnell had insisted on reserving, gave rise to legends and discourses as interminable as the disputes of the schools.

At first Mr. Darnell had proposed that they should furnish the 'spare' room. There were four bedrooms in the house: their own room, the small one for the servant, and two others overlooking the garden, one of which had been used for storing boxes, ends of rope, and odd numbers of 'Quiet Days' and 'Sunday Evenings,' besides some worn suits belonging to Mr. Darnell which had been carefully wrapped up and laid by, as he scarcely knew what to do with them. The other room was frankly waste and vacant, and one Saturday afternoon, as he was coming home in the 'bus, and while he revolved that difficult question of the ten pounds, the unseemly emptiness of the spare room suddenly came into his mind, and he glowed with the idea that now, thanks to Aunt Marian, it could be furnished. He was busied with this delightful thought all the way home, but when he let himself in, he said nothing to his wife, since he felt that his idea must be matured. He told Mrs. Darnell that, having important business, he was obliged to go out again directly, but that he should be back without fail for tea at half-past six; and Mary, on her side, was not sorry to be alone, as she was a little be-hind-hand with the household books. The fact was, that Darnell, full of the design of furnishing the spare bedroom, wished to con-sult his friend Wilson, who lived at Fulham, and had often given him judicious advice as to the laying out of money to the very best advantage. Wilson was connected with the Bordeaux wine trade, and Darnell's only anxiety was lest he should not be at home.

However, it was all right; Darnell took a tram along the Goldhawk Road, and walked the rest of the way, and was delighted to see Wilson in the front garden of his house, busy amongst his flower-beds.

'Haven't seen you for an age,' he said cheerily, when he heard Darnell's hand on the gate; 'come in. Oh, I forgot,' he added, as Darnell still fumbled with the handle, and vainly attempted to enter. 'Of course you can't get in; I haven't shown it you.'

It was a hot day in June, and Wilson appeared in a costume which he had put on in haste as soon as he arrived from the City. He wore a straw hat with a neat pugaree protecting the back of his neck, and his dress was a Norfolk jacket and knickers in heather mixture.

'See,' he said, as he let Darnell in; 'see the dodge. You don't turn the handle at all. First of all push hard, and then pull. It's a trick of my own, and I shall have it patented. You see, it keeps undesirable characters at a distance—such a great thing in the suburbs. I feel I can leave Mrs. Wilson alone now; and, formerly, you have no idea how she used to be pestered.'

'But how about visitors?' said Darnell. 'How do they get in?'

'Oh, we put them up to it. Besides,' he said vaguely, 'there is sure to be somebody looking out. Mrs. Wilson is nearly always at the window. She's out now; gone to call on some friends. The Bennetts' At Home day, I think it is. This is the first Saturday, isn't it? You know J. W. Bennett, don't you? Ah, he's in the House; doing very well, I believe. He put me on to a very good thing the other day.'

'But, I say,' said Wilson, as they turned and strolled towards the front door, 'what do you wear those black things for? You look hot. Look at me. Well, I've been gardening, you know, but I feel as cool as a cucumber. I dare say you don't know where to get these things? Very few men do. Where do you suppose I got 'em?'

'In the West End, I suppose,' said Darnell, wishing to be polite.

'Yes, that's what everybody says. And it is a good cut. Well, I'll tell you, but you needn't pass it on to everybody. I got the tip from Jameson—you know him, "Jim-Jams," in the China trade, 39 Eastbrook—and he said he didn't want everybody in the City to know about it. But just go to Jennings, in Old Wall, and mention my name, and you'll be all right. And what d'you think they cost?'

'I haven't a notion,' said Darnell, who had never bought such a suit in his life.

'Well, have a guess.'

Darnell regarded Wilson gravely. The jacket hung about his body like a sack, the knickerbockers drooped lamentably over his calves, and in prominent positions the bloom of the heather seemed about to fade and disappear.

'Three pounds, I suppose, at least,' he said at length.

'Well, I asked Dench, in our place, the other day, and he guessed four ten, and his father's got something to do with a big business in Conduit Street. But I only gave thirty-five and six. To measure? Of course; look at the cut, man.'

Darnell was astonished at so low a price.

'And, by the way,' Wilson went on, pointing to his new brown boots, 'you know where to go for shoe-leather? Oh, I thought everybody was up to that! There's only one place. "Mr. Bill," in Gunning Street,—nine and six.

They were walking round and round the garden, and Wilson pointed out the flowers in the beds and borders. There were hardly any blossoms, but everything was neatly arranged.

'Here are the tuberous-rooted Glasgownias,' he said, showing a rigid row of stunted plants; 'those are Squintaceæ; this is a new introduction, Moldavia Semperflorida Andersonii; and this is Prattsia'

'When do they come out?' said Darnell.

'Most of them in the end of August or beginning of September,' said Wilson briefly. He was slightly annoyed with himself for having talked so much about his plants, since he saw that Darnell cared nothing for flowers; and, indeed, the visitor could hardly dissemble vague recollections that came to him; thoughts of an old, wild garden, full of odours, beneath grey walls, of the fragrance of the meadowsweet beside the brook.

'I wanted to consult you about some furniture,' Darnell said at last. 'You know we've got a spare room, and I'm thinking of putting a few things into it. I haven't exactly made up my mind, but I thought you might advise me.'

'Come into my den,' said Wilson. 'No; this way, by the back'; and he showed Darnell another ingenious arrangement at the side door whereby a violent high-toned bell was set pealing in the house if one did but touch the latch. Indeed, Wilson handled it so briskly that the bell rang a wild alarm, and the servant, who was trying on her mistress's things in the bedroom, jumped madly to the window and then danced a hysteric dance. There was plaster found on the drawing-room table on Sunday afternoon, and Wilson wrote a letter to the 'Fulham Chronicle,' ascribing the phenomenon 'to some disturbance of a seismic nature.'

For the moment he knew nothing of the great results of his contrivance, and solemnly led the way towards the back of the house. Here there was a patch of turf, beginning to look a little brown, with a background of shrubs. In the middle of the turf, a boy of nine or ten was standing all alone, with something of an air.

'The eldest,' said Wilson. 'Havelock. Well, Lockie, what are ye doing now? And where are your brother and sister?'

The boy was not at all shy. Indeed, he seemed eager to explain the course of events.

'I'm playing at being Gawd,' he said, with an engaging frankness. 'And I've sent Fergus and Janet to the bad place. That's in the shrubbery. And they're never to come out any more. And they're burning for ever and ever.'

'What d'you think of that?' said Wilson admiringly. 'Not bad for a youngster of nine, is it? They think a lot of him at the Sunday-school. But come into my den.'

The den was an apartment projecting from the back of the house. It had been designed as a back kitchen and washhouse, but Wilson had draped the 'copper' in art muslin and had boarded over the sink, so that it served as a workman's bench.

'Snug, isn't it?' he said, as he pushed forward one of the two wicker chairs. 'I think out things here, you know; it's quiet. And what about this furnishing? Do you want to do the thing on a grand scale?'

'Oh, not at all. Quite the reverse. In fact, I don't know whether the sum at our disposal will be sufficient. You see the spare room is ten feet by twelve, with a western exposure, and I thought if we could manage it, that it would seem more cheerful furnished. Besides, it's pleasant to be able to ask a visitor; our aunt, Mrs. Nixon, for example. But she is accustomed to have everything very nice.'

'And how much do you want to spend?'

'Well, I hardly think we should be justified in going much beyond ten pounds. That isn't enough, eh?'

Wilson got up and shut the door of the back kitchen impressively.

'Look here,' he said, 'I'm glad you came to me in the first place. Now you'll just tell me where you thought of going yourself.'

'Well, I had thought of the Hampstead Road,' said Darnell in a hesitating manner.

'I just thought you'd say that. But I'll ask you, what is the good of going to those expensive shops in the West End? You don't get a better article for your money. You're merely paying for fashion.'

'I've seen some nice things in Samuel's, though. They get a brilliant polish on their goods in those superior shops. We went there when we were married.'

'Exactly, and paid ten per cent more than you need have paid. It's throwing money away. And how much did you say you had to spend? Ten pounds. Well, I can tell you where to get a beautiful bedroom suite, in the very highest finish, for six pound ten. What d'you think of that? China included, mind you; and a square of carpet, brilliant colours, will only cost you fifteen and six. Look here, go any Saturday afternoon to Dick's, in the Seven Sisters Road, mention my name, and ask for Mr. Johnston. The suite's in ash, "Elizabethan" they call it. Six pound ten, including the china, with one of their "Orient" carpets, nine by nine, for fifteen and six. Dick's.'

Wilson spoke with some eloquence on the subject of furnishing. He pointed out that the times were changed, and that the old heavy style was quite out of date.

'You know,' he said, 'it isn't like it was in the old days, when people used to buy things to last hundreds of years. Why, just before the wife and I were married, an uncle of mine died up in the

North and left me his furniture. I was thinking of furnishing at the time, and I thought the things might come in handy; but I assure you there wasn't a single article that I cared to give house-room to. All dingy, old mahogany; big bookcases and bureaus, and claw-legged chairs and tables. As I said to the wife (as she was soon afterwards), "We don't exactly want to set up a chamber of horrors, do we?" So I sold off the lot for what I could get. I must confess I like a cheerful room.'

Darnell said he had heard that artists liked the old-fashioned furniture.

'Oh, I dare say. The "unclean cult of the sunflower," eh? You saw that piece in the "Daily Post"? I hate all that rot myself. It isn't healthy, you know, and I don't believe the English people will stand it. But talking of curiosities, I've got something here that's worth a bit of money.'

He dived into some dusty receptacle in a corner of the room, and showed Darnell a small, worm-eaten Bible, wanting the first five chapters of Genesis and the last leaf of the Apocalypse.

It bore the date of 1753.

'It's my belief that's worth a lot,' said Wilson. 'Look at the worm-holes. And you see it's "imperfect," as they call it. You've noticed that some of the most valuable books are "imperfect" at the sales?'

The interview came to an end soon after, and Darnell went home to his tea. He thought seriously of taking Wilson's advice, and after tea he told Mary of his idea and of what Wilson had said about Dick's.

Mary was a good deal taken by the plan when she had heard all the details. The prices struck her as very moderate. They were sitting one on each side of the grate (which was concealed by a pretty cardboard screen, painted with landscapes), and she rested her cheek on her hand, and her beautiful dark eyes seemed to dream and behold strange visions. In reality she was thinking of Darnell's plan.

'It would be very nice in some ways,' she said at last. 'But we must talk it over. What I am afraid of is that it will come to much more than ten pounds in the long run. There are so many things to be considered. There's the bed. It would look shabby if we got a common bed without brass mounts. Then the bedding, the mattress, and blankets, and sheets, and counterpane would all cost something.'

She dreamed again, calculating the cost of all the necessaries, and Darnell stared anxiously; reckoning with her, and wondering what her conclusion would be. For a moment the delicate colouring of her face, the grace of her form, and the brown hair, drooping over her ears and clustering in little curls about her neck, seemed to hint at a language which he had not yet learned; but she spoke again.

'The bedding would come to a great deal, I am afraid. Even if Dicks are considerably cheaper than Boons or Samuels. And, my dear, we must have some ornaments on the mantelpiece. I saw some very nice vases at eleven-three the other day at Wilkin and Dodd's. We should want six at least, and there ought to be a centre-piece. You see how it mounts up.'

Darnell was silent. He saw that his wife was summing up against his scheme, and though he had set his heart on it, he could not resist her arguments.

'It would be nearer twelve pounds than ten,' she said.

'The floor would have to be stained round the carpet (nine by nine, you said?), and we should want a piece of linoleum to go under the washstand. And the walls would look very bare without any pictures.'

'I thought about the pictures,' said Darnell; and he spoke quite eagerly. He felt that here, at least, he was unassailable. 'You know there's the "Derby Day" and the "Railway Station," ready framed, standing in the corner of the box-room already. They're a bit old-fashioned, perhaps, but that doesn't matter in a bedroom.

And couldn't we use some photographs? I saw a very neat frame in natural oak in the City, to hold half a dozen, for one and six. We might put in your father, and your brother James, and Aunt Marian, and your grandmother, in her widow's cap— and any of the others in the album. And then there's that old family picture in the hair-trunk— that might do over the mantelpiece.'

'You mean your great-grandfather in the gilt frame? But that's very old-fashioned, isn't it? He looks so queer in his wig. I don't think it would quite go with the room, somehow.'

Darnell thought a moment. The portrait was a 'kitcat' of a young gentleman, bravely dressed in the fashion of 1750, and he very faintly remembered some old tales that his father had told him about this ancestor—tales of the woods and fields, of the deep sunken lanes, and the forgotten country in the west.

'No,' he said, 'I suppose it is rather out of date. But I saw some very nice prints in the City, framed and quite cheap.'

'Yes, but everything counts. Well, we will talk it over, as you say. You know we must be careful.'

The servant came in with the supper, a tin of biscuits, a glass of milk for the mistress, and a modest pint of beer for the master, with a little cheese and butter. Afterwards Edward smoked two pipes of honeydew, and they went quietly to bed; Mary going first, and her husband following a quarter of an hour later, according to the ritual established from the first days of their marriage. Front and back doors were locked, the gas was turned off at the meter, and when Darnell got upstairs he found his wife already in bed, her face turned round on the pillow.

She spoke softly to him as he came into the room.

'It would be impossible to buy a presentable bed at anything under one pound eleven, and good sheets are dear, anywhere.'

He slipped off his clothes and slid gently into bed, putting out the candle on the table. The blinds were all evenly and duly drawn, but it was a June night, and beyond the walls, beyond that desolate world and wilderness of grey Shepherd's Bush, a great golden moon had floated up through magic films of cloud, above the hill, and the earth was filled with a wonderful light between red sunset lingering over the mountain and that marvelous glory that shone into the woods from the summit of the hill. Darnell seemed to see some reflection of that wizard brightness in the room; the pale walls and the white bed and his wife's face lying amidst brown hair upon the pillow were illuminated, and listening he could almost hear the corncrake in the fields, the fern-owl sounding his strange note from the quiet of the rugged place where the bracken grew, and, like the echo of a magic song, the melody of the nightingale that sang all night in the alder by the little brook. There was nothing that he could say, but he slowly stole his arm under his wife's neck, and played with the ringlets of brown hair. She never moved, she lay there gently breathing, looking up to the blank ceiling of the room with her beautiful eyes, thinking also, no doubt, thoughts that she could not utter, kissing her husband obediently when he asked her to do so, and he stammered and hesitated as he spoke.

They were nearly asleep, indeed Darnell was on the very eve of dreaming, when she said very softly— 'I am afraid, darling, that we could never afford it.' And he heard her words through the murmur of the water, dripping from the grey rock, and falling into the clear pool beneath.

Sunday morning was always an occasion of idleness. Indeed, they would never have got breakfast if Mrs. Darnell, who had the instincts of the housewife, had not awoke and seen the bright sunshine, and felt that the house was too still. She lay quiet for five minutes, while her husband slept beside her, and listened intently, waiting for the sound of Alice stirring down below. A golden tube of sunlight shone through some opening in the Venetian blinds, and it shone on the brown hair that lay about her head on the pillow, and she looked steadily into the room at the 'duchesse' toilet-table, the coloured ware of the washstand, and the two photogra-

vures in oak frames, 'The Meeting' and 'The Parting,' that hung
upon the wall. She was half dreaming as she listened for the servant's footsteps, and the faint shadow of a shade of a thought
came over her, and she imagined dimly, for the quick moment of a
dream, another world where rapture was wine, where one wandered in a deep and happy valley, and the moon was always rising
red above the trees. She was thinking of Hampstead, which represented to her the vision of the world beyond the walls, and the
thought of the heath led her away to Bank Holidays, and then to
Alice. There was not a sound in the house; it might have been
midnight for the stillness if the drawling cry of the Sunday paper
had not suddenly echoed round the corner of Edna Road, and with
it came the warning clank and shriek of the milkman with his pails.

Mrs. Darnell sat up, and wide awake, listened more intently.
The girl was evidently fast asleep, and must be roused, or all the
work of the day would be out of joint, and she remembered how
Edward hated any fuss or discussion about household matters,
more especially on a Sunday, after his long week's work in the City.
She gave her husband an affectionate glance as he slept on, for she
was very fond of him, and so she gently rose from the bed and
went in her nightgown to call the maid.

The servant's room was small and stuffy, the night had
been very hot, and Mrs. Darnell paused for a moment at the door,
wondering whether the girl on the bed was really the dusty-faced
servant who bustled day by day about the house, or even the
strangely bedizened creature, dressed in purple, with a shiny face,
who would appear on the Sunday afternoon, bringing in an early
tea, because it was her 'evening out.' Alice's hair was black and her
skin was pale, almost of the olive tinge, and she lay asleep, her head
resting on one arm, reminding Mrs. Darnell of a queer print of a
'Tired Bacchante' that she had seen long ago in a shop window in
Upper Street, Islington. And a cracked bell was ringing; that meant
five minutes to eight, and nothing done.

She touched the girl gently on the shoulder, and only smiled when her eyes opened, and, waking with a start, she got up in sudden confusion. Mrs. Darnell went back to her room and dressed slowly while her husband still slept, and it was only at the last moment, as she fastened her cherry-coloured bodice, that she roused him, telling him that the bacon would be overdone unless he hurried over his dressing.

Over the breakfast they discussed the question of the spare room all over again. Mrs. Darnell still admitted that the plan of furnishing it attracted her, but she could not see how it could be done for the ten pounds, and as they were prudent people they did not care to encroach on their swings. Edward was highly paid, having (with allowances for extra work in busy weeks) a hundred and forty pounds a year, and Mary had inherited from an old uncle, her godfather, three hundred pounds, which had been judiciously laid out in mortgage at 4½ per cent. Their total income, then, counting in Aunt Marian's present, was a hundred and fifty-eight pounds a year and they were clear of debt, since Darnell had bought the furniture for the house out of money which he had saved for five or six years before. In the first few years of his life in the City his income had, of course, been smaller, and at first he had lived very freely, without a thought of laying by. The theatres and music-halls had attracted him, and scarcely a week passed without his going (in the pit) to one or the other; and he had occasionally bought photographs of actresses who pleased him. These he had solemnly burnt when he became engaged to Mary; he remembered the evening well; his heart had been so full of joy and wonder, and the landlady had complained bitterly of the mess in the grate when he came home from the City the next night.

Still, the money was lost, as far as he could recollect, ten or twelve shillings; and it annoyed him all the more to reflect that if he had put it by, it would have gone far towards the purchase of an 'Orient' carpet in brilliant colours. Then there had been other expenses of his youth: he had purchased threepenny and even four-penny cigars, the latter rarely, but the former frequently, sometimes singly, and sometimes in bundles of twelve for half-a-crown. Once a meerschaum pipe had haunted him for six weeks; the tobacconist had drawn it out of a drawer with some air of secrecy as be was buying a packet of 'Lone Star.' Here was another useless expense, these American-manufactured tobaccos: his 'Lone Star,' 'Long Judge,' 'Old Hank,' 'Sultry Clime,' and the rest of them cost from a shilling to one and six the two-ounce packet; whereas now he got excellent loose honeydew for threepence halfpenny an ounce. But the crafty tradesman, who had marked him down as a buyer of ex-pensive fancy goods, nodded with his air of mystery, and, snapping open the case, displayed the meerschaum before the dazzled eyes of Darnell. The bowl was carved in the likeness of a female figure, showing the head and torso, and the mouthpiece was of the very best amber—only twelve and six, the man said, and the amber alone, he declared, was worth more than that. He explained that he felt some delicacy about showing the pipe to any but a regular cus-tomer, and was willing to take a little under cost price and 'cut the loss.' Darnell resisted for the time, but the pipe troubled him, and at last he bought it. He was pleased to show it to the younger men in the office for a while, but it never smoked very well, and he gave it away just before his marriage, as from the nature of the carving it would have been impossible to use it in his wife's presence. Once, while he was taking his holidays at Hastings, he had purchased a malacca cane—a useless thing that had cost seven shillings—and he reflected with sorrow on the innumerable evenings on which he had rejected his landlady's plain fried chop, and had gone out to flaner among the Italian restaurants in Upper Street, Islington (he lodged in Holloway), pampering himself with expensive delicacies: cutlets and green peas, braised beef with tomato sauce, fillet steak and chipped potatoes, ending the banquet very often with a small wedge of Gruyère, which cost two pence. One night, after receiving a rise in his salary, he had actually drunk a quarter-flask of Chianti and had added the enormities of Benedictine, coffee, and cigarettes to an expenditure already disgraceful, and sixpence to the waiter made the bill amount to four shillings instead of the shilling that would have provided him with a wholesome and sufficient repast at home. Oh, there were many other items in this account of extravagance, and Darnell had often regretted his way of life, thinking that if he had been more careful, five or six pounds a year might have been added to their income.

And the question of the spare room brought back these regrets in an exaggerated degree. He persuaded himself that the extra five pounds would have given a sufficient margin for the outlay that he desired to make; though this was, no doubt, a mistake on his part. But he saw quite clearly that, under the present conditions, there must be no levies made on the very small sum of money that they had saved. The rent of the house was thirty-five, and rates and taxes added another ten pounds—nearly a quarter of their income for houseroom. Mary kept down the housekeeping bills to the very best of her ability, but meat was always dear, and she suspected the maid of cutting surreptitious slices from the joint and eating them in her bedroom with bread and treacle in the dead of night, for the girl had disordered and eccentric appetites. Mr. Darnell thought no more of restaurants, cheap or dear; he took his lunch with him to the City, and joined his wife in the evening at high tea—chops, a bit of steak, or cold meat from the Sunday's dinner.

Mrs. Darnell ate bread and jam and drank a little milk in the middle of the day; but, with the utmost economy, the effort to live within their means and to save for future contingencies was a very hard one. They had determined to do without change of air for at least three years, as the honeymoon at Walton-on-the-Naze had cost a good deal; and it was on this ground that they had, somewhat illogically, reserved the ten pounds, declaring that as they were not to have any holiday they would spend the money on something useful.

And it was this consideration of utility that was finally fatal to Darnell's scheme. They had calculated and recalculated the expense of the bed and bedding, the linoleum, and the ornaments, and by a great deal of exertion the total expenditure had been made to assume the shape of 'something very little over ten pounds,' when Mary said quite suddenly—'But, after all, Edward, we don't really want to furnish the room at all. I mean it isn't necessary. And if we did so it might lead to no end of expense. People would hear of it and be sure to fish for invitations. You know we have relatives in the country, and they would be almost certain, the Mallings, at any rate, to give hints.'

Darnell saw the force of the argument and gave way. But he was bitterly disappointed.

'It would have been very nice, wouldn't it?' he said with a sigh.

'Never mind, dear,' said Mary, who saw that he was a good deal cast down. 'We must think of some other plan that will be nice and useful too.'

She often spoke to him in that tone of a kind mother, though she was by three years the younger.

'And now,' she said, 'I must get ready for church. Are you coming?'

Darnell said that he thought not. He usually accompanied his wife to morning service, but that day he felt some bitterness in his heart, and preferred to lounge under the shade of the big mulberry tree that stood in the middle of their patch of garden—relic of the spacious lawns that had once lain smooth and green and sweet, where the dismal streets now swarmed in a hopeless labyrinth.

So Mary went quietly and alone to church. St. Paul's stood in a neighbouring street, and its Gothic design would have interested a curious inquirer into the history of a strange revival.

Obviously, mechanically, there was nothing amiss. The style chosen was 'geometrical decorated,' and the tracery of the windows seemed correct. The nave, the aisles, the spacious chancel, were reasonably proportioned; and, to be quite serious, the only feature obviously wrong was the substitution of a low 'chancel wall' with iron gates for the rood screen with the loft and rood. But this, it might plausibly be contended, was merely an adaptation of the old idea to modern requirements, and it would have been quite difficult to explain why the whole building, from the mere mortar setting between the stones to the Gothic gas standards, was a mysterious and elaborate blasphemy. The canticles were sung to Joll in B flat, the chants were 'Anglican,' and the sermon was the gospel for the day, amplified and rendered into the more modern and graceful English of the preacher. And Mary came away.

After their dinner (an excellent piece of Australian mutton, bought in the 'World Wide' Stores, in Hammersmith), they sat for some time in the garden, partly sheltered by the big mulberry tree from the observation of their neighbours. Edward smoked his honeydew, and Mary looked at him with placid affection.

'You never tell me about the men in your office,' she said at length. 'Some of them are nice fellows, aren't they?'

'Oh, yes, they're very decent. I must bring some of them round, one of these days.'

He remembered with a pang that it would be necessary to provide whisky. One couldn't ask the guest to drink table beer at ten pence the gallon.

'Who are they, though?' said Mary. 'I think they might have given you a wedding present.'

'Well, I don't know. We never have gone in for that sort of thing. But they're very decent chaps. Well, there's Harvey; "Sauce" they call him behind his back. He's mad on bicycling. He went in last year for the Two Miles Amateur Record. He'd have made it, too, if he could have got into better training.'

'Then there's James, a sporting man. You wouldn't care for him. I always think he smells of the stable.'

'How horrid!' said Mrs. Darnell, finding her husband a little frank, lowering her eyes as she spoke.

'Dickenson might amuse you,' Darnell went on. 'He's always got a joke. A terrible liar, though. When he tells a tale we never know how much to believe. He swore the other day he'd seen one of the governors buying cockles off a barrow near London Bridge, and Jones, who's just come, believed every word of it.'

Darnell laughed at the humorous recollection of the jest.

'And that wasn't a bad yarn about Salter's wife,' he went on. 'Salter is the manager, you know.

Dickenson lives close by, in Notting Hill, and he said one morning that he had seen Mrs. Salter, in the Portobello Road, in red stockings, dancing to a piano organ.'

'He's a little coarse, isn't he?' said Mrs. Darnell. 'I don't see much fun in that.'

'Well, you know, amongst men it's different. You might like Wallis; he's a tremendous photographer. He often shows us photos he's taken of his children—one, a little girl of three, in her bath. I asked him how he thought she'd like it when she was twenty-three.'

Mrs. Darnell looked down and made no answer.

There was silence for some minutes while Darnell smoked his pipe. 'I say, Mary,' he said at length, 'what do you say to our taking a paying guest?'

'A paying guest! I never thought of it. Where should we put him?'

'Why, I was thinking of the spare room. The plan would obviate your objection, wouldn't it? Lots of men in the City take them, and make money of it too. I dare say it would add ten pounds a year to our income. Redgrave, the cashier, finds it worth his while to take a large house on purpose. They have a regular lawn for tennis and a billiard-room.'

Mary considered gravely, always with the dream in her eyes. 'I don't think we could manage it, Edward,' she said; 'it would be inconvenient in many ways. She hesitated for a moment. 'And I don't think I should care to have a young man in the house. It is so very small, and our accommodation, as you know, is so limited.'

She blushed slightly, and Edward, a little disappointed as he was, looked at her with a singular longing, as if he were a scholar confronted with a doubtful hieroglyph, either wholly wonderful or altogether commonplace. Next door children were playing in the garden, playing shrilly, laughing crying, quarrelling, racing to and fro. Suddenly a dear, pleasant voice sounded from an upper window.

'Enid! Charles! Come up to my room at once!'

There was an instant sudden hush. The children's voices died away.

'Mrs. Parker is supposed to keep her children in great order,' said Mary. 'Alice was telling me about it the other day. She had been talking to Mrs. Parker's servant. I listened to her without any remark, as I don't think it right to encourage servants' gossip; they always exaggerate everything. And I dare say children often require to be corrected.'

The children were struck silent as if some ghastly terror had seized them.

Darnell fancied that he heard a queer sort of cry from the house, but could not be quite sure. He turned to the other side, where an elderly, ordinary man with a grey moustache was strolling up and down on the further side of his garden. He caught Darnell's eye, and Mrs. Darnell looking towards him at the same moment, he very politely raised his tweed cap. Darnell was surprised to see his wife blushing fiercely.

'Sayce and I often go into the City by the same 'bus,' he said, 'and as it happens we've sat next to each other two or three times lately. I believe he's a traveler for a leather firm in Bermondsey. He struck me as a pleasant man. Haven't they got rather a good-looking servant?'

'Alice has spoken to me about her—and the Sayces,' said Mrs. Darnell. 'I understand that they are not very well thought of in the neighbourhood. But I must go in and see whether the tea is ready. Alice will be wanting to go out directly.' Darnell looked after his wife as she walked quickly away. He only dimly understood, but he could see the charm of her figure, the delight of the brown curls clustering about her neck, and he again felt that sense of the scholar confronted by the hieroglyphic. He could not have expressed his emotion, but he wondered whether he would ever find the key, and something told him that before she could speak to him his own lips must be unclosed. She had gone into the house by the back kitchen door, leaving it open, and he heard her speaking to the girl about the water being 'really boiling.' He was amazed, almost indignant with himself; but the sound of the words came to his ears as strange, heart-piercing music, tones from another, wonderful sphere. And yet he was her husband, and they had been married nearly a year; and yet, whenever she spoke, he had to listen to the sense of what she said, constraining himself, lest he should believe she was a magic creature, knowing the secrets of immeasurable delight.

He looked out through the leaves of the mulberry tree. Mr. Sayce had disappeared from his view, but he saw the light-blue fume of the cigar that he was smoking floating slowly across the shadowed air. He was wondering at his wife's manner when Sayce's name was mentioned, puzzling his head as to what could be amiss in the household of a most respectable personage, when his wife appeared at the dining-room window and called him in to tea. She smiled as he looked up, and he rose hastily and walked in, wondering whether he were not a little 'queer,' so strange were the dim emotions and the dimmer impulses that rose within him.

Alice was all shining purple and strong scent, as she brought in the teapot and the jug of hot water. It seemed that a visit to the kitchen had inspired Mrs. Darnell in her turn with a novel plan for disposing of the famous ten pounds. The range had always been a trouble to her, and when sometimes she went into the kitchen, and found, as she said, the fire 'roaring halfway up the chimney,' it was in vain that she reproved the maid on the ground of extravagance and waste of coal. Alice was ready to admit the absurdity of making up such an enormous fire merely to bake (they called it 'roast') a bit of beef or mutton, and to boil the potatoes and the cabbage; but she was able to show Mrs. Darnell that the fault lay in the defective contrivance of the range, in an oven which 'would not get hot.' Even with a chop or a steak it was almost as bad; the heat seemed to escape up the chimney or into the room, and Mary had spoken several times to her husband on the shocking waste of coal, and the cheapest coal procurable was never less than eighteen shillings the ton. Mr. Darnell had written to the landlord, a builder, who had replied in an illiterate but offensive communication, maintaining the excellence of the stove and charging all the faults to the account of 'your good lady,' which really implied that the Darnells kept no servant, and that Mrs. Darnell did everything. The range, then, remained a standing annoyance and expense. Every morning, Alice said, she had the greatest difficulty in getting the fire to light at all, and once lighted it 'seemed as if it fled right up the chimney.' Only a few nights before Mrs. Darnell had spoken seriously to her husband about it; she had got Alice to weigh the coals expended in cooking a cottage pie, the dish of the evening, and deducting what remained in the scuttle after the pie was done, it appeared that the wretched thing had consumed nearly twice the proper quantity of fuel.

'You remember what I said the other night about the range?' said Mrs. Darnell, as she poured out the tea and watered the leaves. She thought the introduction a good one, for though her husband was a most amiable man, she guessed that he had been just a little hurt by her decision against his furnishing scheme.

'The range?' said Darnell. He paused as he helped himself to the marmalade and considered for a moment. 'No, I don't recollect. What night was it?'

'Tuesday. Don't you remember? You had "overtime," and didn't get home till quite late.' She paused for a moment, blushing slightly; and then began to recapitulate the misdeeds of the range, and the outrageous outlay of coal in the preparation of the cottage pie.

'Oh, I recollect now. That was the night I thought I heard the nightingale (people say there are nightingales in Bedford Park), and the sky was such a wonderful deep blue.'

He remembered how he had walked from Uxbridge Road Station, where the green 'bus stopped, and in spite of the fuming kilns under Acton, a delicate odour of the woods and summer fields was mysteriously in the air, and he had fancied that he smelt the red wild roses, drooping from the hedge. As he came to his gate he saw his wife standing in the doorway, with a light in her hand, and he threw his arms violently about her as she welcomed him, and whispered something in her ear, kissing her scented hair. He had felt quite abashed a moment afterwards, and he was afraid that he had frightened her by his nonsense; she seemed trembling and confused. And then she had told him how they had weighed the coal.

'Yes, I remember now,' he said. 'It is a great nuisance, isn't it? I hate to throw away money like that.'

'Well, what do you think? Suppose we bought a really good range with aunt's money? It would save us a lot, and I expect the things would taste much nicer.'

Darnell passed the marmalade, and confessed that the idea was brilliant.

'It's much better than mine, Mary,' he said quite frankly. 'I am so glad you thought of it. But we must talk it over; it doesn't do to buy in a hurry. There are so many makes.'

Each had seen ranges which looked miraculous inventions; he in the neighbourhood of the City; she in Oxford Street and Regent Street, on visits to the dentist. They discussed the matter at tea, and afterwards they discussed it walking round and round the garden, in the sweet cool of the evening.

'They say the "Newcastle" will burn anything, coke even,' said Mary.

'But the "Glow" got the gold medal at the Paris Exhibition,' said Edward.

'But what about the "Eutopia" Kitchener? Have you seen it at work in Oxford Street?' said Mary. 'They say their plan of ventilating the oven is quite unique.'

'I was in Fleet Street the other day,' answered Edward, 'and I was looking at the "Bliss" Patent Stoves. They burn less fuel than any in the market—so the makers declare.'

He put his arm gently round her waist. She did not repel him; she whispered quite softly—'I think Mrs. Parker is at her window,' and he drew his arm back slowly.

'But we will talk it over,' he said. 'There is no hurry. I might call at some of the places near the City, and you might do the same thing in Oxford Street and Regent Street and Piccadilly, and we could compare notes.'

Mary was quite pleased with her husband's good temper. It was so nice of him not to find fault with her plan; 'He's so good to me,' she thought, and that was what she often said to her brother, who did not care much for Darnell. They sat down on the seat under the mulberry, close together, and she let Darnell take her hand, and as she felt his shy, hesitating fingers touch her in the shadow, she pressed them ever so softly, and as he fondled her hand, his breath was on her neck, and she heard his passionate, hesitating voice whisper, 'My dear, my dear,' as his lips touched her cheek. She trembled a little, and waited. Darnell kissed her gently on the cheek and drew away his hand, and when he spoke he was almost breathless.

'We had better go in now,' he said. 'There is a heavy dew, and you might catch cold.'

A warm, scented gale came to them from beyond the walls. He longed to ask her to stay out with him all night beneath the tree, that they might whisper to one another, that the scent of her hair might inebriate him, that he might feel her dress still brushing against his ankles. But he could not find the words, and it was absurd, and she was so gentle that she would do whatever he asked, however foolish it might be, just because he asked her. He was not worthy to kiss her lips; he bent down and kissed her silk bodice, and again he felt that she trembled, and he was ashamed, fearing that he had frightened her.

They went slowly into the house, side by side, and Darnell lit the gas in the drawing-room, where they always sat on Sunday evenings. Mrs. Darnell felt a little tired and lay down on the sofa, and Darnell took the arm-chair opposite. For a while they were silent, and then Darnell said suddenly—'What's wrong with the Sayces? You seemed to think there was something a little strange about them. Their maid looks quite quiet.'

'Oh, I don't know that one ought to pay any attention to servants' gossip. They're not always very truthful.'

'It was Alice told you, wasn't it?'

'Yes. She was speaking to me the other day, when I was in the kitchen in the afternoon.'

'But what was it?'

'Oh, I'd rather not tell you, Edward. It's not pleasant. I scolded Alice for repeating it to me.'

Darnell got up and took a small, frail chair near the sofa.

'Tell me,' he said again, with an odd perversity. He did not really care to hear about the household next door, but he remembered how his wife's cheeks flushed in the afternoon, and now he was looking at her eyes.

'Oh, I really couldn't tell you, dear. I should feel ashamed.'

'But you're my wife.'

'Yes, but it doesn't make any difference. A woman doesn't like to talk about such things.'

Darnell bent his head down. His heart was beating; he put his ear to her mouth and said, 'Whisper.'

Mary drew his head down still lower with her gentle hand, and her cheeks burned as she whispered—'Alice says that—upstairs—they have only—one room furnished. The maid told her—herself.' With an unconscious gesture she pressed his head to her breast, and he in turn was bending her red lips to his own, when a violent jangle clamoured through the silent house. They sat up, and Mrs. Darnell went hurriedly to the door.

'That's Alice,' she said. 'She is always in in time. It has only just struck ten.'

Darnell shivered with annoyance. His lips, he knew, had almost been opened. Mary's pretty handkerchief, delicately scented from a little flagon that a school friend had given her, lay on the floor, and he picked it up, and kissed it, and hid it away.

The question of the range occupied them all through June and far into July. Mrs. Darnell took every opportunity of going to the West End and investigating the capacity of the latest makes, gravely viewing the new improvements and hearing what the shopmen had to say; while Darnell, as he said, 'kept his eyes open' about the City. They accumulated quite a literature of the subject, bringing away illustrated pamphlets, and in the evenings it was an amusement to look at the pictures. They viewed with reverence and interest the drawings of great ranges for hotels and public institutions, mighty contrivances furnished with a series of ovens each for a different use, with wonderful apparatus for grilling, with batteries of accessories which seemed to invest the cook almost with the dignity of a chief engineer. But when, in one of the lists, they encountered the images of little toy 'cottage' ranges, for four pounds, and even for three pounds ten, they grew scornful, on the strength of the eight or ten pound article which they meant to purchase— when the merits of the divers patents had been thoroughly thrashed out.

The 'Raven' was for a long time Mary's favourite. It promised the utmost economy with the highest efficiency, and many times they were on the point of giving the order. But the 'Glow' seemed equally seductive, and it was only £8. 5s. as compared with £9. 7s. 6d., and though the 'Raven' was supplied to the Royal Kitchen, the 'Glow' could show more fervent testimonials from continental potentates.

It seemed a debate without end, and it endured day after day till that morning, when Darnell woke from the dream of the ancient wood, of the fountains rising into grey vapour beneath the heat of the sun. As he dressed, an idea struck him, and he brought it as a shock to the hurried breakfast, disturbed by the thought of the City 'bus which passed the corner of the street at 9.15.

'I've got an improvement on your plan, Mary,' he said, with triumph. 'Look at that,' and he flung a little book on the table.

He laughed. 'It beats your notion all to fits. After all, the great expense is the coal. It's not the stove—at least that's not the real mischief. It's the coal is so dear. And here you are. Look at those oil stoves. They don't burn any coal, but the cheapest fuel in the world—oil; and for two pounds ten you can get a range that will do everything you want.'

'Give me the book,' said Mary, 'and we will talk it over in the evening, when you come home.

'Must you be going?'

Darnell cast an anxious glance at the clock.

'Good-bye,' and they kissed each other seriously and duti-fully, and Mary's eyes made Darnell think of those lonely water-pools, hidden in the shadow of the ancient woods.

So, day after day, he lived in the grey phantasmal world, akin to death, that has, somehow, with most of us, made good its claim to be called life. To Darnell the true life would have seemed mad-ness, and when, now and again, the shadows and vague images reflected from its splendour fell across his path, he was afraid, and took refuge in what he would have called the sane 'reality' of com-mon and usual incidents and interests. His absurdity was, perhaps, the more evident, inasmuch as 'reality' for him was a matter of kitchen ranges, of saving a few shillings; but in truth the folly would have been greater if it had been concerned with racing stables, steam yachts, and the spending of many thousand pounds.

But so went forth Darnell, day by day, strangely mistaking death for life, madness for sanity, and purposeless and wandering phantoms for true beings. He was sincerely of opinion that he was a City clerk, living in Shepherd's Bush—having forgotten the mysteries and the far-shining glories of the kingdom which was his by legitimate inheritance.

# II

All day long a fierce and heavy heat had brooded over the City, and as Darnell neared home he saw the mist lying on all the damp lowlands, wreathed in coils about Bedford Park to the south, and mounting to the West, so that the tower of Acton Church loomed out of a grey lake. The grass in the squares and on the lawns which he overlooked as the 'bus lumbered wearily along was burnt to the colour of dust. Shepherd's Bush Green was a wretched desert, trampled brown, bordered with monotonous poplars, whose leaves hung motionless in air that was still, hot smoke. The foot passengers struggled wearily along the pavements, and the reek of the summer's end mingled with the breath of the brickfields made Darnell gasp, as if he were inhaling the poison of some foul sick-room.

He made but a slight inroad into the cold mutton that adorned the tea-table, and confessed that he felt rather 'done up' by the weather and the day's work.

'I have had a trying day, too,' said Mary. 'Alice has been very queer and troublesome all day, and I have had to speak to her quite seriously. You know I think her Sunday evenings out have a rather unsettling influence on the girl. But what is one to do?'

'Has she got a young man?'

'Of course: a grocer's assistant from the Goldhawk Road—Wilkin's, you know. I tried them when we settled here, but they were not very satisfactory.'

'What do they do with themselves all the evening? They have from five to ten, haven't they?'

'Yes; five, or sometimes half-past, when the water won't boil. Well, I believe they go for walks usually. Once or twice he has taken her to the City Temple, and the Sunday before last they walked up and down Oxford Street, and then sat in the Park. But it seems that last Sunday they went to tea with his mother at Putney. I should like to tell the old woman what I really think of her.'

'Why? What happened? Was she nasty to the girl?'

'No; that's just it. Before this, she has been very unpleasant on several occasions. When the young man first took Alice to see her—that was in March—the girl came away crying; she told me so herself. Indeed, she said she never wanted to see old Mrs. Murry again; and I told Alice that, if she had not exaggerated things, I could hardly blame her for feeling like that.'

'Why? What did she cry for?'

'Well, it seems that the old lady—she lives in quite a small cottage in some Putney back street—was so stately that she would hardly speak. She had borrowed a little girl from some neighbour's family, and had managed to dress her up to imitate a servant, and Alice said nothing could be sillier than to see that mite opening the door, with her black dress and her white cap and apron, and she hardly able to turn the handle, as Alice said. George (that's the young man's name) had told Alice that it was a little bit of a house; but he said the kitchen was comfortable, though very plain and old-fashioned. But, instead of going straight to the back, and sitting by a big fire on the old settle that they had brought up from the country, that child asked for their names (did you ever hear such nonsense?) and showed them into a little poky parlour, where old Mrs. Murry was sitting "like a duchess," by a fireplace full of coloured paper, and the room as cold as ice. And she was so grand that she would hardly speak to Alice.'

'That must have been very unpleasant.'

'Oh, the poor girl had a dreadful time. She began with: "Very pleased to make your acquaintance, Miss Dill. I know so very few persons in service." Alice imitates her mincing way of talking, but I can't do it. And then she went on to talk about her family, how they had farmed their own land for five hundred years—such stuff! George had told Alice all about it: they had had an old cottage with a good strip of garden and two fields somewhere in Essex, and that old woman talked almost as if they had been country gentry, and boasted about the Rector, Dr. Somebody, coming to see them so often, and of Squire Somebody Else always looking them up, as if they didn't visit them out of kindness. Alice told me it was as much as she could do to keep from laughing in Mrs. Murry's face, her young man having told her all about the place, and how small it was, and how the Squire had been so kind about buying it when old Murry died and George was a little boy, and his mother not able to keep things going. However, that silly old woman "laid it on thick," as you say, and the young man got more and more uncomfortable, especially when she went on to speak about marrying in one's own class, and how unhappy she had known young men to be who had married beneath them, giving some very pointed looks at Alice as she talked. And then such an amusing thing happened: Alice had noticed George looking about him in a puzzled sort of way, as if he couldn't make out something or other, and at last he burst out and asked his mother if she had been buying up the neighbours' ornaments, as he remembered the two green cut-glass vases on the mantelpiece at Mrs. Ellis's, and the wax flowers at Miss Turvey's. He was going on, but his mother scowled at him, and upset some books, which he had to pick up; but Alice quite understood she had been borrowing things from her neighbours, just as she had borrowed the little girl, so as to look grander. And then they had tea—water bewitched, Alice calls it—and very thin bread and butter, and rubbishy foreign pastry from the Swiss shop in the High Street—all sour froth and rancid fat, Alice declares. And then Mrs. Murry began boasting again about her family, and snubbing Alice and talking at her, till the girl came away quite furious, and very unhappy, too. I don't wonder at it, do you?'

'It doesn't sound very enjoyable, certainly,' said Darnell, looking dreamily at his wife. He had not been attending very carefully to the subject-matter of her story, but he loved to hear a voice that was incantation in his ears, tones that summoned before him the vision of a magic world.

'And has the young man's mother always been like this?' he said after a long pause, desiring that the music should continue.

'Always, till quite lately, till last Sunday in fact. Of course Alice spoke to George Murry at once, and said, like a sensible girl, that she didn't think it ever answered for a married couple to live with the man's mother, "especially," she went on, "as I can see your mother hasn't taken much of a fancy to me." He told her, in the usual style, it was only his mother's way, that she didn't really mean anything, and so on; but Alice kept away for a long time, and rather hinted, I think, that it might come to having to choose between her and his mother. And so affairs went on all through the spring and summer, and then, just before the August Bank Holiday, George spoke to Alice again about it, and told her how sorry the thought of any unpleasantness made him, and how he wanted his mother and her to get on with each other, and how she was only a bit old-fashioned and queer in her ways, and had spoken very nicely to him about her when there was nobody by. So the long and the short of it was that Alice said she might come with them on the Monday, when they had settled to go to Hampton Court—the girl was always talking about Hampton Court, and wanting to see it. You remember what a beautiful day it was, don't you?'

'Let me see,' said Darnell dreamily. 'Oh yes, of course—I sat out under the mulberry tree all day, and we had our meals there: it was quite a picnic. The caterpillars were a nuisance, but I enjoyed the day very much.' His ears were charmed, ravished with the grave, supernal melody, as of antique song, rather of the first made world in which all speech was descant, and all words were sacraments of might, speaking not to the mind but to the soul. He lay back in his chair, and said—'Well, what happened to them?'

'My dear, would you believe it; but that wretched old woman behaved worse than ever. They met as had been arranged, at Kew Bridge, and got places, with a good deal of difficulty, in one of those char-à-banc things, and Alice thought she was going to enjoy herself tremendously.

Nothing of the kind. They had hardly said "Good morning," when old Mrs. Murry began to talk about Kew Gardens, and how beautiful it must be there, and how much more convenient it was than Hampton, and no expense at all; just the trouble of walking over the bridge. Then she went on to say, as they were waiting for the char-à-banc, that she had always heard there was nothing to see at Hampton, except a lot of nasty, grimy old pictures, and some of them not fit for any decent woman, let alone girl, to look at, and she wondered why the Queen allowed such things to be shown, putting all kinds of notions into girls' heads that were light enough already; and as she said that she looked at Alice so nastily—horrid old thing—that, as she told me afterwards, Alice would have slapped her face if she hadn't been an elderly woman, and George's mother. Then she talked about Kew again, saying how wonderful the hot-houses were, with palms and all sorts of wonderful things, and a lily as big as a parlour table, and the view over the river. George was very good, Alice told me. He was quite taken aback at first, as the old woman had promised faithfully to be as nice as ever she could be; but then he said, gently but firmly, "Well, mother, we must go to Kew some other day, as Alice has set her heart on Hampton for to-day, and I want to see it myself!" All Mrs. Murry did was to snort, and look at the girl like vinegar, and just then the char-à-banc came up, and they had to scramble for their seats. Mrs. Mummy grumbled to herself in an indistinct sort of voice all the way to Hampton Court. Alice couldn't very well make out what she said, but now and then she seemed to hear bits of sentences, like: Pity to grow old, if Sons grow bold; and Honour thy father and mother; and Lie on the shelf, said the housewife to the old shoe, and the wicked son to his mother; and I gave you milk and you give me the go-by.

Alice thought they must be proverbs (except the Commandment, of course), as George was always saying how old-fashioned his mother is; but she says there were so many of them, and all pointed at her and George, that she thinks now Mrs. Murry must have made them up as they drove along. She says it would be just like her to do it, being old-fashioned, and ill-natured too, and fuller of talk than a butcher on Saturday night. Well, they got to Hampton at last, and Alice thought the place would please her, perhaps, and they might have some enjoyment. But she did nothing but grumble, and out loud too, so that people looked at them, and a woman said, so that they could hear, "Ah well, they'll be old themselves some day," which made Alice very angry, for, as she said, they weren't doing anything. When they showed her the chestnut avenue in Bushey Park, she said it was so long and straight that it made her quite dull to look at it, and she thought the deer (you know how pretty they are, really) looked thin and miserable, as if they would be all the better for a good feed of hog-wash, with plenty of meal in it. She said she knew they weren't happy by the look in their eyes, which seemed to tell hem that their keepers beat them. It was the same with everything; she said she remembered market-gardens in Hammersmith and Gunnersbury that had a better show of flowers, and when they took her to the place where the water is, under the trees, she burst out with its being rather hard to tramp her off her legs to show her a common canal, with not so much as a barge on it to liven it up a bit. She went on like that the whole day, and Alice told me she was only too thankful to get home and get rid of her. Wasn't it wretched for the girl?'

'It must have been, indeed. But what happened last Sunday?'

'That's the most extraordinary thing of all. I noticed that Alice was rather queer in her manner this morning; she was a longer time washing up the breakfast things, and she answered me quite sharply when I called to her to ask when she would be ready to help me with the wash; and when I went into the kitchen to see about something, I noticed that she was going about her work in a sulky sort of way. So I asked her what was the matter, and then it all came out. I could scarcely believe my own ears when she mumbled out something about Mrs. Murry thinking she could do very much better for herself; but I asked her one question after another till I had it all out of her.

It just shows one how foolish and empty-headed these girls are. I told her she was no better than a weather-cock. If you will believe me, that horrid old woman was quite another person when Alice went to see her the other night. Why, I can't think, but so she was. She told the girl how pretty she was; what a neat figure she had; how well she walked; and how she'd known many a girl not half so clever or well-looking earning her twenty-five or thirty pounds a year, and with good families. She seems to have gone into all sorts of details, and made elaborate calculations as to what she would be able to save, "with decent folks, who don't screw, and pinch, and lock up everything in the house," and then she went off into a lot of hypocritical nonsense about how fond she was of Alice, and how she could go to her grave in peace, knowing how happy her dear George would be with such a good wife, and about her savings from good wages helping to set up a little home, ending up with "And, if you take an old woman's advice, deary, it won't be long before you hear the marriage bells."

'I see,' said Darnell; 'and the upshot of it all is, I suppose, that the girl is thoroughly dissatisfied?'

'Yes, she is so young and silly. I talked to her, and reminded her of how nasty old Mrs. Murry had been, and told her that she might change her place and change for the worse. I think I have persuaded her to think it over quietly, at all events. Do you know what it is, Edward? I have an idea. I believe that wicked old woman is trying to get Alice to leave us that she may tell her son how changeable she is; and I suppose she would make up some of her stupid old proverbs:

"A changeable wife, a troublesome life," or some nonsense of the kind. Horrid old thing!'

'Well, well,' said Darnell, 'I hope she won't go, for your sake. It would be such a bother for you, hunting for a fresh servant.'

He refilled his pipe and smoked placidly, refreshed somewhat after the emptiness and the burden of the day. The French window was wide open, and now at last there came a breath of quickening air, distilled by the night from such trees as still wore green in that arid valley. The song to which Darnell had listened in rapture, and now the breeze, which even in that dry, grim suburb still bore the word of the woodland, had summoned the dream to his eyes, and he meditated over matters that his lips could not express.

'She must, indeed, be a villainous old woman,' he said at length.

'Old Mrs. Murry? Of course she is; the mischievous old thing! Trying to take the girl from a comfortable place where she is happy.'

'Yes; and not to like Hampton Court! That shows how bad she must be, more than anything.'

'It is beautiful, isn't it?'

'I shall never forget the first time I saw it. It was soon after I went into the City; the first year. I had my holidays in July, and I was getting such a small salary that I couldn't think of going away to the seaside, or anything like that. I remember one of the other men wanted me to come with him on a walking tour in Kent. I should have liked that, but the money wouldn't run to it. And do you know what I did? I lived in Great College Street then, and the first day I was off, I stayed in bed till past dinner-time, and lounged about in an arm-chair with a pipe all the afternoon. I had got a new kind of tobacco—one and four for the two-ounce packet—much dearer than I could afford to smoke, and I was enjoying it immensely. It was awfully hot, and when I shut the window and drew down the red blind it grew hotter; at five o'clock the room was like an oven.

But I was so pleased at not having to go into the City, that I didn't mind anything, and now and again I read bits from a queer old book that had belonged to my poor dad. I couldn't make out what a lot of it meant, but it fitted in somehow, and I read and smoked till tea-time. Then I went out for a walk, thinking I should be better for a little fresh air before I went to bed; and I went wandering away, not much noticing where I was going, turning here and there as the fancy took me. I must have gone miles and miles, and a good many of them mound and round, as they say they do in Australia if they lose their way in the bush; and I am sure I couldn't have gone exactly the same way all over again for any money. Anyhow, I was still in the streets when the twilight came on, and the lamp-lighters were trotting round from one lamp to another. It was a wonderful night: I wish you had been there, my dear.'

'I was quite a little girl then.'

'Yes, I suppose you were. Well, it was a wonderful night. I remember, I was walking in a little street of little grey houses all alike, with stucco copings and stucco door-posts; there were brass plates on a lot of the doors, and one had "Maker of Shell Boxes" on it, and I was quite pleased, as I had often wondered where those boxes and things that you buy at the seaside came from. A few children were playing about in the road with some rubbish or other, and men were singing in a small public-house at the corner, and I happened to look up, and I noticed what a wonderful colour the sky had turned. I have seen it since, but I don't think it has ever been quite what it was that night, a dark blue, glowing like a violet, just as they say the sky looks in foreign countries. I don't know why, but the sky or something made me feel quite queer; everything seemed changed in a way I couldn't understand. I remember, I told an old gentleman I knew then—a friend of my poor father's, he's been dead for five years, if not more—about how I felt, and he looked at me and said something about fairyland; I don't know what he meant, and I dare say I didn't explain myself properly. But, do you know, for a moment or two I felt as if that little back street was beautiful, and the noise of the children and the men in the public-house seemed to fit in with the sky and become part of it. You know that old saying about "treading on air" when one is glad!

'Well, I really felt like that as I walked, not exactly like air, you know, but as if the pavement was velvet or some very soft carpet. And then—I suppose it was all my fancy—the air seemed to smell sweet, like the incense in Catholic churches, and my breath came queer and catchy, as it does when one gets very excited about anything. I felt altogether stranger than I've ever felt before or since.'

Darnell stopped suddenly and looked up at his wife. She was watching him with parted lips, with eager, wondering eyes.

'I hope I'm not tiring you, dear, with all this story about nothing. You have had a worrying day with that stupid girl; hadn't you better go to bed?'

'Oh, no, please, Edward. I'm not a bit tired now. I love to hear you talk like that. Please go on.'

'Well, after I had walked a bit further, that queer sort of feeling seemed to fade away. I said a bit further, and I really thought I had been walking about five minutes, but I had looked at my watch just before I got into that little street, and when I looked at it again it was eleven o'clock. I must have done about eight miles. I could scarcely believe my own eyes, and I thought my watch must have gone mad; but I found out afterwards it was perfectly right. I couldn't make it out, and I can't now; I assure you the time passed as if I walked up one side of Edna Road and down the other. But there I was, right in the open country, with a cool wind blowing on me from a wood, and the air full of soft rustling sounds, and notes of birds from the bushes, and the singing noise of a little brook that ran under the road. I was standing on the bridge when I took out my watch and struck a wax light to see the time; and it came upon me suddenly what a strange evening it had been. It was all so different, you see, to what I had been doing all my life, particularly for the year before, and it almost seemed as if I couldn't be the man who had been going into the City every day in the morning and coming back from it every evening after writing a lot of uninteresting letters. It was like being pitched all of a sudden from one world into another. Well, I found my way back somehow or other, and as I went along I made up my mind how I'd spend my holiday. I said to myself, "I'll have a walking tour as well as Ferrars, only mine is to be a tour of London and its environs," and I had got it all settled when I let myself into the house about four o'clock in the morning, and the sun was shining, and the street almost as still as the wood at midnight!'

'I think that was a capital idea of yours. Did you have your tour? Did you buy a map of London?'

'I had the tour all right. I didn't buy a map; that would have spoilt it, somehow; to see everything plotted out, and named, and measured. What I wanted was to feel that I was going where nobody had been before. That's nonsense, isn't it? as if there could be any such places in London, or England either, for the matter of that.'

'I know what you mean; you wanted to feel as if you were going on a sort of voyage of discovery. Isn't that it?'

'Exactly, that's what I was trying to tell you. Besides, I didn't want to buy a map. I made a map.'

'How do you mean? Did you make a map out of your head?'

'I'll tell you about it afterwards. But do you really want to hear about my grand tour?'

'Of course I do; it must have been delightful. I call it a most original idea.'

'Well, I was quite full of it, and what you said just now about a voyage of discovery reminds me of how I felt then. When I was a boy I was awfully fond of reading of great travelers—I suppose all boys are—and of sailors who were driven out of their course and found themselves in latitudes where no ship had ever sailed before, and of people. who discovered wonderful cities in strange countries; and all the second day of my holidays I was feeling just as I used to when I read these books. I didn't get up till pretty late. I was tired to death after all those miles I had walked; but when I had finished my breakfast and filled my pipe, I had a grand time of it. It was such nonsense, you know; as if there could be anything strange or wonderful in London.'

'Why shouldn't there be?'

'Well, I don't know; but I have thought afterwards what a silly lad I must have been. Anyhow, I had a great day of it, planning what I would do, half making-believe—just like a kid—that I didn't know where I might find myself, or what might happen to me. And I was enormously pleased to think it was all my secret, that nobody else knew anything about it, and that, whatever I might see, I would keep to myself. I had always felt like that about the books. Of course, I loved reading them, but it seemed to me that, if I had been a discoverer, I would have kept my discoveries a secret. If I had been Columbus, and, if it could possibly have been managed, I would have found America all by myself, and never have said a word about it to anybody.

Fancy! How beautiful it would be to be walking about in one's own town, and talking to people, and all the while to have the thought that one knew of a great world beyond the seas, that nobody else dreamed of. I should have loved that!

'And that is exactly what I felt about the tour I was going to make. I made up my mind that nobody should know; and so, from that day to this, nobody has heard a word of it.'

'But you are going to tell me?'

'You are different. But I don't think even you will hear everything; not because I won't, but because I can't tell many of the things I saw.'

'Things you saw? Then you really did see wonderful, strange things in London?'

'Well, I did and I didn't. Everything, or pretty nearly everything, that I saw is standing still, and hundreds of thousands of people have looked at the same sights—there were many places that the fellows in the office knew quite well, I found out afterwards. And then I read a book called "London and its Surroundings." But (I don't know how it is) neither the men at the office nor the writers of the book seem to have seen the things that I did. That's why I stopped reading the book; it seemed to take the life, the real heart, out of everything, making it as dry and stupid as the stuffed birds in a museum.

'I thought about what I was going to do all that day, and went to bed early, so as to be fresh. I knew wonderfully little about London, really; though, except for an odd week now and then, I had spent all my life in town. Of course I knew the main streets—the Strand, Regent Street, Oxford Street, and so on—and I knew the way to the school I used to go to when I was a boy, and the way into the City. But I had just kept to a few tracks, as they say the sheep do on the mountains; and that made it all the easier for me to imagine that I was going to discover a new world.'

Darnell paused in the stream of his talk. He looked keenly at his wife to see if he were wearying her, but her eyes gazed at him with unabated interest—one would have almost said that they were the eyes of one who longed and half expected to be initiated into the mysteries, who knew not what great wonder was to be revealed. She sat with her back to the open window, framed in the sweet dusk of the night, as if a painter had made a curtain of heavy velvet behind her; and the work that she had been doing had fallen to the floor. She supported her head with her two hands placed on each side of her brow, and her eyes were as the wells in the wood of which Darnell dreamed in the night-time and in the day.

'And all the strange tales I had ever heard were in my head that morning,' he went on, as if continuing the thoughts that had filled his mind while his lips were silent. 'I had gone to bed early, as I told you, to get a thorough rest, and I had set my alarum clock to wake me at three, so that I might set out at an hour that was quite strange for the beginning of a journey. There was a hush in the world when I awoke, before the clock had rung to arouse me, and then a bird began to sing and twitter in the elm tree that grew in the next garden, and I looked out of the window, and everything was still, and the morning air breathed in pure and sweet, as I had never known it before. My room was at the back of the house, and most of the gardens had trees in them, and beyond these trees I could see the backs of the houses of the next street rising like the wall of an old city; and as I looked the sun rose, and the great light came in at my window, and the day began.

'And I found that when I was once out of the streets just about me that I knew, some of the queer feeling that had come to me two days before came back again. It was not nearly so strong, the streets no longer smelt of incense, but still there was enough of it to show me what a strange world I passed by. There were things that one may see again and again in many London streets: a vine or a fig tree on a wall, a lark singing in a cage, a curious shrub blossoming in a garden, an odd shape of a roof, or a balcony with an uncommon-looking trellis-work in iron. There's scarcely a street, perhaps, where you won't see one or other of such things as these; but that morning they rose to my eyes in a new light, as if I had on the magic spectacles in the fairy tale, and just like the man in the fairy tale, I went on and on in the new light. I remember going through wild land on a high place; there were pools of water shining in the sun, and great white houses in the middle of dark, rocking pines, and then on the turn of the height I came to a little lane that went aside from the main road, a lane that led to a wood, and in the lane was a little old shadowed house, with a bell turret in the roof, and a porch of trellis-work all dim and faded into the colour of the sea; and in the garden there were growing tall, white lilies, just as we saw them that day we went to look at the old pictures; they were shining like silver, and they filled the air with their sweet scent. It was from near that house I saw the valley and high places far away in the sun. So, as I say, I went "on and on," by woods and fields, till I came to a little town on the top of a hill, a town full of old houses bowing to the ground beneath their years, and the morning was so still that the blue smoke rose up straight into the sky from all the roof-tops, so still that I heard far down in the valley the song of a boy who was singing an old song through the streets as he went to school, and as I passed through the awakening town, beneath the old, grave houses, the church bells began to ring.

'It was soon after I had left this town behind me that I found the Strange Road. I saw it branching off from the dusty high road, and it looked so green that I turned aside into it, and soon I felt as if I had really come into a new country. I don't know whether it was one of the roads the old Romans made that my father used to tell me about; but it was covered with deep, soft turf, and the great tall hedges on each side looked as if they had not been touched for a hundred years; they had grown so broad and high and wild that they met overhead, and I could only get glimpses here and there of the country through which I was passing, as one passes in a dream. The Strange Road led me on and on, up and down hill; sometimes the rose bushes had grown so thick that I could scarcely make my way between them, and sometimes the road broadened out into a green, and in one valley a brook, spanned by an old wooden bridge, ran across it. I was tired, and I found a soft and shady place beneath an ash tree, where I must have slept for many hours, for when I woke up it was late in the afternoon. So I went on again, and at last the green road came out into the highway, and I looked up and saw another town on a high place with a great church in the middle of it, and when I went up to it there was a great organ sounding from within, and the choir was singing.'

There was a rapture in Darnell's voice as he spoke, that made his story well-nigh swell into a song, and he drew a long breath as the words ended, filled with the thought of that far-off summer day, when some enchantment had informed all common things, transmuting them into a great sacrament, causing earthly works to glow with the fire and the glory of the everlasting light.

And some splendour of that light shone on the face of Mary as she sat still against the sweet gloom of the night, her dark hair making her face more radiant. She was silent for a little while, and then she spoke—'Oh, my dear, why have you waited so long to tell me these wonderful things? I think it is beautiful. Please go on.'

'I have always been afraid it was all nonsense,' said Darnell. 'And I don't know how to explain what I feel. I didn't think I could say so much as I have to-night.'

'And did you find it the same day after day?'

'All through the tour? Yes, I think every journey was a success. Of course, I didn't go so far afield every day; I was too tired.

Often I rested all day long, and went out in the evening, after the lamps were lit, and then only for a mile or two. I would roam about old, dim squares, and hear the wind from the hills whispering in the trees; and when I knew I was within call of some great glittering street, I was sunk in the silence of ways where I was almost the only passenger, and the lamps were so few and faint that they seemed to give out shadows instead of light. And I would walk slowly, to and fro, perhaps for an hour at a time, in such dark streets, and all the time I felt what I told you about its being my secret—that the shadow, and the dim lights, and the cool of the evening, and trees that were like dark low clouds were all mine, and mine alone, that I was living in a world that nobody else knew of, into which no one could enter.

'I remembered one night I had gone farther. It was somewhere in the far west, where there are orchards and gardens, and great broad lawns that slope down to trees by the river. A great red moon rose that night through mists of sunset, and thin, filmy clouds, and I wandered by a road that passed through the orchards, till I came to a little hill, with the moon showing above it glowing like a great rose. Then I saw figures pass between me and the moon, one by one, in a long line, each bent double, with great packs upon their shoulders. One of them was singing, and then in the middle of the song I heard a horrible shrill laugh, in the thin cracked voice of a very old woman, and they disappeared into the shadow of the trees. I suppose they were people going to work, or coming from work in the gardens; but how like it was to a nightmare! I can't tell you about Hampton; I should never finish talking. I was there one evening, not long before they closed the gates, and there were very few people about. But the grey-red, silent, echoing courts, and the flowers falling into dreamland as the night came on, and the dark yews and shadowy-looking statues, and the far, still stretches of water beneath the avenues; and all melting into a blue mist, all being hidden from one's eyes, slowly, surely, as if veils were dropped, one by one, on a great ceremony! Oh! my dear, what could it mean? Far away, across the river, I heard a soft bell ring three times, and three times, and again three times, and I turned away, and my eyes were full of tears.

'I didn't know what it was when I came to it; I only found out afterwards that it must have been Hampton Court. One of the men in the office told me he had taken an A. B. C. girl there, and they had great fun. They got into the maze and couldn't get out again, and then they went on the river and were nearly drowned. He told me there were some spicy pictures in the galleries; his girl shrieked with laughter, so he said.'

Mary quite disregarded this interlude.

'But you told me you had made a map. What was it like?'

'I'll show it you some day, if you want to see it. I marked down all the places I had gone to, and made signs—things like queer letters—to remind me of what I had seen. Nobody but myself could understand it. I wanted to draw pictures, but I never learnt how to draw, so when I tried nothing was like what I wanted it to be. I tried to draw a picture of that town on the hill that I came to on the evening of the first day; I wanted to make a steep hill with houses on top, and in the middle, but high above them, the great church, all spires and pinnacles, and above it, in the air, a cup with rays coming from it. But it wasn't a success. I made a very strange sign for Hampton Court, and gave it a name that I made up out of my head.'

The Darnells avoided one another's eyes as they sat at breakfast the next morning. The air had lightened in the night, for rain had fallen at dawn; and there was a bright blue sky, with vast white clouds rolling across it from the south-west, and a fresh and joyous wind blew in at the open window; the mists had vanished. And with the mists there seemed to have vanished also the sense of strange things that had possessed Mary and her husband the night before; and as they looked out into the clear light they could scarcely believe that the one had spoken and the other had listened a few hours before to histories very far removed from the usual current of their thoughts and of their lives. They glanced shyly at one another, and spoke of common things, of the question whether Alice would be corrupted by the insidious Mrs. Murry, or whether Mrs. Darnell would be able to persuade the girl that the old woman must be actuated by the worst motives.

'And I think, if I were you,' said Darnell, as he went out, 'I should step over to the stores and complain of their meat. That last piece of beef was very far from being up to the mark—full of sinew.'

# III

It might have been different in the evening, and Darnell had matured a plan by which he hoped to gain much. He intended to ask his wife if she would mind having only one gas, and that a good deal lowered, on the pretext that his eyes were tired with work; he thought many things might happen if the room were dimly lit, and the window opened, so that they could sit and watch the night, and listen to the rustling murmur of the tree on the lawn. But his plans were made in vain, for when he got to the garden gate his wife, in tears, came forth to meet him.

'Oh, Edward,' she began, 'such a dreadful thing has happened! I never liked him much, but I didn't think he would ever do such awful things.'

'What do you mean? Who are you talking about? What has happened? Is it Alice's young man?'

'No, no. But come in, dear. I can see that woman opposite watching us: she's always on the look out.'

'Now, what is it?' said Darnell, as they sat down to tea. 'Tell me, quick! you've quite frightened me.'

'I don't know how to begin, or where to start. Aunt Marian

has thought that there was something queer for weeks. And then she found—oh, well, the long and short of it is that Uncle Robert has been carrying on dreadfully with some horrid girl, and aunt has found out everything!'

'Lord! you don't say so! The old rascal! Why, he must be nearer seventy than sixty!'

'He's just sixty-five; and the money he has given her—'

The first shock of surprise over, Darnell turned resolutely to his mince.

'We'll have it all out after tea,' he said; 'I am not going to have my meals spoilt by that old fool of a Nixon. Fill up my cup, will you, dear?'

'Excellent mince this,' he went on, calmly. 'A little lemon juice and a bit of ham in it? I thought there was something extra. Alice all right to-day? That's good. I expect she's getting over all that nonsense.'

He went on calmly chattering in a manner that astonished Mrs. Darnell, who felt that by the fall of Uncle Robert the natural order had been inverted, and had scarcely touched food since the intelligence had arrived by the second post. She had started out to keep the appointment her aunt had made early in the morning, and had spent most of the day in a first-class waiting-room at Victoria Station, where she had heard all the story.

'Now,' said Darnell, when the table had been cleared, 'tell us all about it. How long has it been going on?'

'Aunt thinks now, from little things she remembers, that it must have been going on for a year at least. She says there has been a horrid kind of mystery about uncle's behaviour for a long time, and her nerves were quite shaken, as she thought he must be involved with Anarchists, or something dreadful of the sort.'

'What on earth made her think that?'

"Well, you see, once or twice when she was out walking with her husband, she has been startled by whistles, which seemed to follow them everywhere. You know there are some nice country walks at Barnet, and one in particular, in the fields near Totteridge, that uncle and aunt rather made a point of going to on fine Sunday evenings. Of course, this was not the first thing she noticed, but, at the time, it made a great impression on her mind; she could hardly get a wink of sleep for weeks and weeks.'

'Whistling?' said Darnell. 'I don't quite understand. Why should she be frightened by whistling?'

'I'll tell you. The first time it happened was one Sunday in last May. Aunt had a fancy they were being followed a Sunday or two before, but she didn't see or hear anything, except a sort of crackling noise in the hedge. But this particular Sunday they had hardly got through the stile into the fields, when she heard a peculiar kind of low whistle. She took no notice, thinking it was no concern of hers or her husband's, but as they went on she heard it again, and then again, and it followed them the whole walk, and it made her so uncomfortable, because she didn't know where it was coming from or who was doing it, or why. Then, just as they got out of the fields into the lane, uncle said he felt quite faint, and he thought he would try a little brandy at the "Turpin's Head," a small public-house there is there. And she looked at him and saw his face was quite purple—more like apoplexy, as she says, than fainting fits, which make people look a sort of greenish-white. But she said nothing, and thought perhaps uncle had a peculiar way of fainting of his own, as he always was a man to have his own way of doing everything. So she just waited in the road, and he went ahead and slipped into the public, and aunt says she thought she saw a little figure rise out of the dusk and slip in after him, but she couldn't be sure. And when uncle came out he looked red instead of purple, and said he felt much better; and so they went home quietly together, and nothing more was said. You see, uncle had said nothing about the whistling, and aunt had been so frightened that she didn't dare speak, for fear they might be both shot.

# Arthur Machen

'She wasn't thinking anything more about it, when two Sundays afterwards the very same thing happened just as it had before. This time aunt plucked up a spirit, and asked uncle what it could be. And what do you think he said? "Birds, my dear, birds." Of course aunt said to him that no bird that ever flew with wings made a noise like that: sly, and low, with pauses in between; and then he said that many rare sorts of birds lived in North Middlesex and Hertfordshire. "Nonsense, Robert," said aunt, "how can you talk so, considering it has followed us all the way, for a mile or more?" And then uncle told her that some birds were so attached to man that they would follow one about for miles sometimes; he said he had just been reading about a bird like that in a book of travels. And do you know that when they got home he actually showed her a piece in the "Hertfordshire Naturalist" which they took in to oblige a friend of theirs, all about rare birds found in the neighbourhood, all the most outlandish names, aunt says, that she had never heard or thought of, and uncle had the impudence to say that it must have been a Purple Sandpiper, which, the paper said, had "a low shrill note, constantly repeated." And then he took down a book of Siberian Travels from the bookcase and showed her a page which told how a man was followed by a bird all day long through a forest. And that's what Aunt Marian says vexes her more than anything almost; to think that he should be so artful and ready with those books, twisting them to his own wicked ends. But, at the time, when she was out walking, she simply couldn't make out what he meant by talking about birds in that random, silly sort of way, so unlike him, and they went on, that horrible whistling following them, she looking straight ahead and walking fast, really feeling more huffy and put out than frightened. And when they got to the next stile, she got over and turned round, and "lo and behold," as she says, there was no Uncle Robert to be seen! She felt herself go quite white with alarm, thinking of that whistle, and making sure he'd been spirited away or snatched in some way or another, and she had just screamed out "Robert" like a mad woman, when he came quite slowly round the corner, as cool as a cucumber, holding something in his hand. He said there were some flowers he could never pass, and when aunt saw that he had got a dandelion torn up by the roots, she felt as if her head were going round.'

Mary's story was suddenly interrupted. For ten minutes Darnell had been writhing in his chair, suffering tortures in his anxiety to avoid wounding his wife's feelings, but the episode of the dandelion was too much for him, and he burst into a long, wild shriek of laughter, aggravated by suppression into the semblance of a Red Indian's war-whoop. Alice, who was washing-up in the scullery, dropped some three shillings' worth of china, and the neighbours ran out into their gardens wondering if it were murder. Mary gazed reproachfully at her husband.

'How can you be so unfeeling, Edward?' she said, at length, when Darnell had passed into the feebleness of exhaustion. 'If you had seen the tears rolling down poor Aunt Marian's cheeks as she told me, I don't think you would have laughed. I didn't think you were so hard-hearted.'

'My dear Mary,' said Darnell, faintly, through sobs and catching of the breath, 'I am awfully sorry. I know it's very sad, really, and I'm not unfeeling; but it is such an odd tale, now, isn't it? The Sandpiper, you know, and then the dandelion!'

His face twitched and he ground his teeth together. Mary looked gravely at him for a moment, and then she put her hands to her face, and Darnell could see that she also shook with merriment.

'I am as bad as you,' she said, at last. 'I never thought of it in that way. I'm glad I didn't, or I should have laughed in Aunt Marian's face, and I wouldn't have done that for the world. Poor old thing; she cried as if her heart would break. I met her at Victoria, as she asked me, and we had some soup at a confectioner's. I could scarcely touch it; her tears kept dropping into the plate all the time; and then we went to the waiting-room at the station, and she cried there terribly.'

'Well,' said Darnell, 'what happened next? I won't laugh any more.

'No, we mustn't; it's much too horrible for a joke. Well, of course aunt went home and wondered and wondered what could be the matter, and tried to think it out, but, as she says, she could make nothing of it. She began to be afraid that uncle's brain was giving way through overwork, as he had stopped in the City (as he said) up to all hours lately, and he had to go to Yorkshire (wicked old story-teller!), about some very tiresome business connected with his leases. But then she reflected that however queer he might be getting, even his queerness couldn't make whistles in the air, though, as she said, he was always a wonderful man. So she had to give that up; and then she wondered if there were anything the matter with her, as she had read about people who heard noises when there was really nothing at all. But that wouldn't do either, because though it might account for the whistling, it wouldn't account for the dandelion or the Sandpiper, or for fainting fits that turned purple, or any of uncle's queerness. So aunt said she could think of nothing but to read the Bible every day from the beginning, and by the time she got into Chronicles she felt rather better, especially as nothing had happened for three or four Sundays. She noticed uncle seemed absent-minded, and not as nice to her as he might be, but she put that down to too much work, as he never came home before the last train, and had a hansom twice all the way, getting there between three and four in the morning. Still, she felt it was no good bothering her head over what couldn't be made out or explained anyway, and she was just settling down, when one Sunday evening it began all over again, and worse things happened. The whistling followed them just as it did before, and poor aunt set her teeth and said nothing to uncle, as she knew he would only tell her stories, and they were walking on, not saying a word, when something made her look back, and there was a horrible boy with red hair, peeping through the hedge just behind, and grinning. She said it was a dreadful face, with something unnatural about it, as if it had been a dwarf, and before she had time to have a good look, it popped back like lightning, and aunt all but fainted away.'

'A red-headed boy?' said Darnell. 'I thought—What an extraordinary story this is. I've never heard of anything so queer. Who was the boy?'

'You will know in good time,' said Mrs. Darnell. 'It is very strange, isn't it?'

'Strange!' Darnell ruminated for a while.

'I know what I think, Mary,' he said at length. 'I don't believe a word of it. I believe your aunt is going mad, or has gone mad, and that she has delusions. The whole thing sounds to me like the invention of a lunatic.'

'You are quite wrong. Every word is true, and if you will let me go on, you will understand how it all happened.'

'Very good, go ahead.'

'Let me see, where was I? Oh, I know, aunt saw the boy grinning in the hedge. Yes, well, she was dreadfully frightened for a minute or two; there was something so queer about the face, but then she plucked up a spirit and said to herself, "After all, better a boy with red hair than a big man with a gun," and she made up her mind to watch Uncle Robert closely, as she could see by his look he knew all about it; he seemed as if he were thinking hard and puzzling over something, as if he didn't know what to do next, and his mouth kept opening and shutting, like a fish's. So she kept her face straight, and didn't say a word, and when he said something to her about the fine sunset, she took no notice. "Don't you hear what I say, Marian?" he said, speaking quite crossly, and bellowing as if it were to somebody in the next field. So aunt said she was very sorry, but her cold made her so deaf, she couldn't hear much. She noticed uncle looked quite pleased, and relieved too, and she knew he thought she hadn't heard the whistling. Suddenly uncle pretended to see a beautiful spray of honeysuckle high up in the hedge, and he said he must get it for aunt, only she must go on ahead, as it made him nervous to be watched. She said she would, but she just stepped aside behind a bush where there was a sort of cover in the hedge, and found she could see him quite well, though she scratched her face terribly with poking it into a rose bush. And in a minute or two out came the boy from behind the hedge, and she saw uncle and him talking, and she knew it was the same boy, as it wasn't dark enough to hide his flaming red head. And uncle put out his hand as if to catch him, but he just darted into the bushes and vanished. Aunt never said a word at the time, but that night when they got home she charged uncle with what she'd seen and asked him what it all meant. He was quite taken aback at first, and stammered and stuttered and said a spy wasn't his notion of a good wife, but at last he made her swear secrecy, and told her that he was a very high Freemason, and that the boy was an emissary of the order who brought him messages of the greatest importance. But aunt didn't believe a word of it, as an uncle of hers was a mason, and he never behaved like that. It was then she began to be afraid that it was really Anarchists, or something of the kind, and every time the bell rang she thought that uncle had been found out, and the police had come for him.'

'What nonsense! As if a man with house property would be an Anarchist.'

'Well, she could see there must be some horrible secret, and she didn't know what else to think. And then she began to have the things through the post.'

'Things through the post! What do you mean by that?'

'All sorts of things; bits of broken bottle-glass, packed carefully as if it were jewellery; parcels that unrolled and unrolled worse than Chinese boxes, and then had "cat" in large letters when you came to the middle; old artificial teeth, a cake of red paint, and at last cockroaches.'

'Cockroaches by post! Stuff and nonsense; your aunt's mad.'

'Edward, she showed me the box; it was made to hold cigarettes, and there were three dead cockroaches inside. And when she found a box of exactly the same kind, half-full of cigarettes, in uncle's great-coat pocket, then her head began to turn again.'

Darnell groaned, and stirred uneasily in his chair, feeling that the tale of Aunt Marian's domestic troubles was putting on the semblance of an evil dream.

'Anything else?' he asked.

'My dear, I haven't repeated half the things poor aunt told me this afternoon. There was the night she thought she saw a ghost in the shrubbery. She was anxious about some chickens that were just due to hatch out, so she went out after dark with some egg and bread-crumbs, in case they might be out. And just before her she saw a figure gliding by the rhododendrons. It looked like a short, slim man dressed as they used to be hundreds of years ago; she saw the sword by his side, and the feather in his cap. She thought she should have died, she said, and though it was gone in a minute, and she tried to make out it was all her fancy, she fainted when she got into the house. Uncle was at home that night, and when she came to and told him he ran out, and stayed out for half-an-hour or more, and then came in and said he could find nothing; and the next minute aunt heard that low whistle just outside the window, and uncle ran out again.'

'My dear Mary, do let us come to the point. What on earth does it all lead to?'

'Haven't you guessed? Why, of course it was that girl all the time.'

'Girl? I thought you said it was a boy with a red head?'

'Don't you see? She's an actress, and she dressed up. She won't leave uncle alone. It wasn't enough that he was with her nearly every evening in the week, but she must be after him on Sundays too. Aunt found a letter the horrid thing had written, and so it has all come out. Enid Vivian she calls herself, though I don't suppose she has any right to one name or the other. And the question is, what is to be done?'

'Let us talk of that again. I'll have a pipe, and then we'll go to bed.'

They were almost asleep when Mary said suddenly—'Doesn't it seem queer, Edward? Last night you were telling me such beautiful things, and to-night I have been talking about that disgraceful old man and his goings on.'

'I don't know,' answered Darnell, dreamily. 'On the walls of that great church upon the hill I saw all kinds of strange grinning monsters, carved in stone.'

The misdemeanours of Mr. Robert Nixon brought in their train consequences strange beyond imagination. It was not that they continued to develop on the somewhat fantastic lines of these first adventures which Mrs. Darnell had related; indeed, when 'Aunt Marian' came over to Shepherd's Bush, one Sunday afternoon, Darnell wondered how he had had the heart to laugh at the misfortunes of a broken-hearted woman.

He had never seen his wife's aunt before, and he was strangely surprised when Alice showed her into the garden where they were sitting on the warm and misty Sunday in September. To him, save during these latter days, she had always been associated with ideas of splendour and success: his wife had always mentioned the Nixons with a tinge of reverence; he had heard, many times, the epic of Mr. Nixon's struggles and of his slow but triumphant rise. Mary had told the story as she had received it from her parents, beginning with the flight to London from some small, dull, and unprosperous town in the flattest of the Midlands, long ago, when a young man from the country had great chances of fortune. Robert Nixon's father had been a grocer in the High Street, and in after days the successful coal merchant and builder loved to tell of that dull provincial life, and while he glorified his own victories, he gave his hearers to understand that he came of a race which had also known how to achieve. That had been long ago, he would explain: in the days when that rare citizen who desired to go to London or to York was forced to rise in the dead of night, and make his way, somehow or other, by ten miles of quagmirish, wandering lanes to the Great North Road, there to meet the 'Lightning' coach, a vehicle which stood to all the countryside as the visible and tangible embodiment of tremendous speed—'and indeed,' as Nixon would add, 'it was always up to time, which is more than can be said of the Dunham Branch Line nowadays!' It was in this ancient Dunham that the Nixons had waged successful trade for perhaps a hundred years, in a shop with bulging bay windows looking on the market-place.

There was no competition, and the townsfolk, and well-to-do farmers, the clergy and the country families, looked upon the house of Nixon as an institution fixed as the town hall (which stood on Roman pillars) and the parish church. But the change came: the railway crept nearer and nearer, the farmers and the country gentry became less well-to-do; the tanning, which was the local industry, suffered from a great business which had been established in a larger town, some twenty miles away, and the profits of the Nixons grew less and less. Hence the hegira of Robert, and he would dilate on the poorness of his beginnings, how he saved, by little and little, from his sorry wage of City clerk, and how he and a fellow clerk, 'who had come into a hundred pounds,' saw an opening in the coal trade—and filled it. It was at this stage of Robert's fortunes, still far from magnificent, that Miss Marian Reynolds had encountered him, she being on a visit to friends in Gunnersbury. Afterwards, victory followed victory; Nixon's wharf became a landmark to bargemen; his power stretched abroad, his dusky fleets went outwards to the sea, and inward by all the far reaches of canals. Lime, cement, and bricks were added to his merchandise, and at last be hit upon the great stroke—that extensive taking up of land in the north of London. Nixon himself ascribed this coup to native sagacity, and the possession of capital; and there were also obscure rumours to the effect that someone or other had been 'done' in the course of the transaction. However that might be, the Nixons grew wealthy to excess, and Mary had often told her husband of the state in which they dwelt, of their liveried servants, of the glories of their drawing-room, of their broad lawn, shadowed by a splendid and ancient cedar.

And so Darnell had somehow been led into conceiving the lady of this demesne as a personage of no small pomp. He saw her, tall, of dignified port and presence, inclining, it might be, to some measure of obesity, such a measure as was not unbefitting in an elderly lady of position, who lived well and lived at ease. He even imagined a slight ruddiness of complexion, which went very well with hair that was beginning to turn grey, and when he heard the door-bell ring, as he sat under the mulberry on the Sunday afternoon, he bent forward to catch sight of this stately figure, clad, of course, in the richest, blackest silk, girt about with heavy chains of gold.

He started with amazement when he saw the strange presence that followed the servant into the garden. Mrs. Nixon was a little, thin old woman, who bent as she feebly trotted after Alice; her eyes were on the ground, and she did not lift them when the Darnells rose to greet her. She glanced to the right, uneasily, as she shook hands with Darnell, to the left when Mary kissed her, and when she was placed on the garden seat with a cushion at her back, she looked away at the back of the houses in the next street. She was dressed in black, it was true, but even Darnell could see that her gown was old and shabby, that the fur trimming of her cape and the fur boa which was twisted about her neck were dingy and disconsolate, and had all the melancholy air which fur wears when it is seen in a second-hand clothes-shop in a back street. And her gloves— they were black kid, wrinkled with much wear, faded to a bluish hue at the finger-tips, which showed signs of painful mending. Her hair, plastered over her forehead, looked dull and colourless, though some greasy matter had evidently been used with a view of producing a becoming gloss, and on it perched an antique bonnet, adorned with black pendants that rattled paralytically one against the other.

And there was nothing in Mrs. Nixon's face to correspond with the imaginary picture that Darnell had made of her. She was sallow, wrinkled, pinched; her nose ran to a sharp point, and her red-rimmed eyes were a queer water-grey, that seemed to shrink alike from the light and from encounter with the eyes of others. As she sat beside his wife on the green garden-seat, Darnell, who occupied a wicker-chair brought out from the drawing-room, could not help feeling that this shadowy and evasive figure, muttering replies to Mary's polite questions, was almost impossibly remote from his conceptions of the rich and powerful aunt, who could give away a hundred pounds as a mere birthday gift. She would say little at first; yes, she was feeling rather tired, it had been so hot all the way, and she had been afraid to put on lighter things as one never knew at this time of year what it might be like in the evenings; there were apt to be cold mists when the sun went down, and she didn't care to risk bronchitis.

'I thought I should never get here,' she went on, raising her voice to an odd querulous pipe.

'I'd no notion it was such an out-of-the-way place, it's so many years since I was in this neighbourhood.'

She wiped her eyes, no doubt thinking of the early days at Turnham Green, when she married Nixon; and when the pocket-handkerchief had done its office she replaced it in a shabby black bag which she clutched rather than carried. Darnell noticed, as he watched her, that the bag seemed full, almost to bursting, and he speculated idly as to the nature of its contents: correspondence, perhaps, he thought, further proofs of Uncle Robert's treacherous and wicked dealings. He grew quite uncomfortable, as he sat and saw her glancing all the while furtively away from his wife and himself, and presently he got up and strolled away to the other end of the garden, where he lit his pipe and walked to and fro on the gravel walk, still astounded at the gulf between the real and the imagined woman.

Presently he heard a hissing whisper, and he saw Mrs. Nixon's head inclining to his wife's.

Mary rose and came towards him.

'Would you mind sitting in the drawing-room, Edward?' she murmured. 'Aunt says she can't bring herself to discuss such a delicate matter before you. I dare say it's quite natural.'

'Very well, but I don't think I'll go into the drawing-room. I feel as if a walk would do me good. You mustn't be frightened if I am a little late,' he said; 'if I don't get back before your aunt goes, say good-bye to her for me.'

He strolled into the main road, where the trains were humming to and fro. He was still confused and perplexed, and he tried to account for a certain relief he felt in removing himself from the presence of Mrs. Nixon. He told himself that her grief at her husband's ruffianly conduct was worthy of all pitiful respect, but at the same time, to his shame, he had felt a certain physical aversion from her as she sat in his garden in her dingy black, dabbing her red-rimmed eyes with a damp pocket-handkerchief. He had been to the Zoo when he was a lad, and he still remembered how he had shrunk with horror at the sight of certain reptiles slowly crawling over one another in their slimy pond. But he was enraged at the similarity between the two sensations, and he walked briskly on that level and monotonous road, looking about him at the unhandsome spectacle of suburban London keeping Sunday.

There was something in the tinge of antiquity which still exists in Acton that soothed his mind and drew it away from those unpleasant contemplations, and when at last he had penetrated rampant after rampart of brick, and heard no more the harsh shrieks and laughter of the people who were enjoying themselves, he found a way into a little sheltered field, and sat down in peace beneath a tree, whence he could look out on a pleasant valley. The sun sank down beneath the hills, the clouds changed into the likeness of blossoming rose-gardens; and he still sat there in the gathering darkness till a cool breeze blew upon him, and he rose with a sigh, and turned back to the brick ramparts and the glimmering streets, and the noisy idlers sauntering to and fro in the procession of their dismal festival. But he was murmuring to himself some words that seemed a magic song, and it was with uplifted heart that he let himself into his house.

Mrs. Nixon had gone an hour and a half before his return, Mary told him. Darnell sighed with relief, and he and his wife strolled out into the garden and sat down side by side.

They kept silence for a time, and at last Mary spoke, not without a nervous tremor in her voice.

'I must tell you, Edward,' she began, 'that aunt has made a proposal which you ought to hear. I think we should consider it.'

'A proposal? But how about the whole affair? Is it still going on?'

'Oh, yes! She told me all about it. Uncle is quite unrepentant. It seems he has taken a flat somewhere in town for that woman, and furnished it in the most costly manner. He simply laughs at aunt's reproaches, and says he means to have some fun at last. You saw how broken she was?'

'Yes; very sad. But won't he give her any money? Wasn't she very badly dressed for a woman in her position?'

'Aunt has no end of beautiful things, but I fancy she likes to hoard them; she has a horror of spoiling her dresses. It isn't for want of money, I assure you, as uncle settled a very large sum on her two years ago, when he was everything that could be desired as a husband. And that brings me to what I want to say. Aunt would like to live with us. She would pay very liberally. What do you say?'

'Would like to live with us?' exclaimed Darnell, and his pipe dropped from his hand on to the grass. He was stupefied by the thought of Aunt Marian as a boarder, and sat staring vacantly before him, wondering what new monster the night would next produce.

'I knew you wouldn't much like the idea,' his wife went on. 'But I do think, dearest, that we ought not to refuse without very serious consideration. I am afraid you did not take to poor aunt very much.'

Darnell shook his head dumbly.

'I thought you didn't; she was so upset, poor thing, and you didn't see her at her best. She is really so good. But listen to me, dear. Do you think we have the right to refuse her offer? I told you she has money of her own, and I am sure she would be dreadfully offended if we said we wouldn't have her. And what would become of me if anything happened to you? You know we have very little saved.'

Darnell groaned.

'It seems to me,' he said, 'that it would spoil everything. We are so happy, Mary dear, by ourselves. Of course I am extremely sorry for your aunt. I think she is very much to be pitied.

'But when it comes to having her always here—'

'I know, dear. Don't think I am looking forward to the prospect; you know I don't want anybody but you. Still, we ought to think of the future, and besides we shall be able to live so very much better. I shall be able to give you all sorts of nice things that I know you ought to have after all that hard work in the City. Our income would be doubled.'

'Do you mean she would pay us £150 a year?'

'Certainly. And she would pay for the spare room being furnished, and any extra she might want. She told me, specially, that if a friend or two came now and again to see her, she would gladly bear the cost of a fire in the drawing-room, and give something towards the gas bill, with a few shillings for the girl for any additional trouble. We should certainly be more than twice as well off as we are now. You see, Edward, dear, it's not the sort of offer we are likely to have again. Besides, we must think of the future, as I said. Do you know aunt took a great fancy to you?'

He shuddered and said nothing, and his wife went on with her argument.

'And, you see, it isn't as if we should see so very much of her. She will have her breakfast in bed, and she told me she would often go up to her room in the evening directly after dinner. I thought that very nice and considerate. She quite understands that we shouldn't like to have a third person always with us. Don't you think, Edward, that, considering everything, we ought to say we will have her?'

'Oh, I suppose so,' he groaned. 'As you say, it's a very good offer, financially, and I am afraid it would be very imprudent to refuse. But I don't like the notion, I confess.'

'I am so glad you agree with me, dear. Depend upon it, it won't be half so bad as you think.

'And putting our own advantage on one side, we shall really be doing poor aunt a very great kindness. Poor old dear, she cried bitterly after you were gone; she said she had made up her mind not to stay any longer in Uncle Robert's house, and she didn't know where to go, or what would become of her, if we refused to take her in. She quite broke down.'

'Well, well; we will try it for a year, anyhow. It may be as you say; we shan't find it quite so bad as it seems now. Shall we go in?'

He stooped for his pipe, which lay as it had fallen, on the grass. He could not find it, and lit a wax match which showed him the pipe, and close beside it, under the seat, something that looked like a page torn from a book. He wondered what it could be, and picked it up.

The gas was lit in the drawing-room, and Mrs. Darnell, who was arranging some notepaper, wished to write at once to

Mrs. Nixon, cordially accepting her proposal, when she was startled by an exclamation from her husband.

'What is the matter?' she said, startled by the tone of his voice. 'You haven't hurt yourself?'

'Look at this,' he replied, handing her a small leaflet; 'I found it under the garden seat just now.'

Mary glanced with bewilderment at her husband and read as follows.

## THE NEW AND CHOSEN SEED OF ABRAHAM
PROPHECIES TO BE FULFILLED IN THE PRESENT YEAR

1. The Sailing of a Fleet of One hundred and Forty and Four Vessels for Tarshish and the Isles.

2. Destruction of the Power of the Dog, including all the instruments of anti-Abrahamic legislation.

3. Return of the Fleet from Tarshish, bearing with it the gold of Arabia, destined to be the Foundation of the New City of Abraham.

4. The Search for the Bride, and the bestowing of the Seals on the Seventy and Seven.

5. The Countenance of FATHER to become luminous, but with a greater glory than the face of Moses.

6. The Pope of Rome to be stoned with stones in the valley called Berek-Zittor.

7. FATHER to be acknowledged by Three Great Rulers. Two Great Rulers will deny FATHER, and will immediately perish in the Effluvia of FATHER'S Indignation.

8. Binding of the Beast with the Little Horn, and all Judges cast down.

9. Finding of the Bride in the Land of Egypt, which has been revealed to FATHER as now existing in the western part of London.

10. Bestowal of the New Tongue on the Seventy and Seven, and on the One Hundred and Forty and Four. FATHER proceeds to the Bridal Chamber.

11. Destruction of London and rebuilding of the City called No, which is the New City of Abraham.

12. FATHER united to the Bride, and the present Earth removed to the Sun for the space of half an hour.

Mrs. Darnell's brow cleared as she read matter which seemed to her harmless if incoherent.

From her husband's voice she had been led to fear something more tangibly unpleasant than a vague catena of prophecies.

'Well,' she said, 'what about it?'

'What about it? Don't you see that your aunt dropped it, and that she must be a raging lunatic?'

'Oh, Edward! don't say that. In the first place, how do you know that aunt dropped it at all? It might easily have blown over from any of the other gardens.

And, if it were hers, I don't think you should call her a lunatic. I don't believe, myself, that there are any real prophets now; but there are many good people who think quite differently. I knew an old lady once who, I am sure, was very good, and she took in a paper every week that was full of prophecies and things very like this. Nobody called her mad, and I have heard father say that she had one of the sharpest heads for business he had ever come across.'

'Very good; have it as you like. But I believe we shall both be sorry.'

They sat in silence for some time. Alice came in after her 'evening out,' and they sat on, till Mrs. Darnell said she was tired and wanted to go to bed.

Her husband kissed her. 'I don't think I will come up just yet,' he said; 'you go to sleep, dearest. I want to think things over. No, no; I am not going to change my mind: your aunt shall come, as I said. But there are one or two things I should like to get settled in my mind.'

# Arthur Machen

He meditated for a long while, pacing up and down the room. Light after light was extinguished in Edna Road, and the people of the suburb slept all around him, but still the gas was alight in Darnell's drawing-room, and he walked softly up and down the floor. He was thinking that about the life of Mary and himself, which had been so quiet, there seemed to be gathering on all sides grotesque and fantastic shapes, omens of confusion and disorder, threats of madness; a strange company from another world. It was as if into the quiet, sleeping streets of some little ancient town among the hills there had come from afar the sound of drum and pipe, snatches of wild song, and there had burst into the market-place the mad company of the players, strangely bedizened, dancing a furious measure to their hurrying music, drawing forth the citizens from their sheltered homes and peaceful lives, and alluring them to mingle in the significant figures of their dance.

Yet afar and near (for it was hidden in his heart) he beheld the glimmer of a sure and constant star. Beneath, darkness came on, and mists and shadows closed about the town. The red, flickering flame of torches was kindled in the midst of it. The song grew louder, with more insistent, magical tones, surging and falling in unearthly modulations, the very speech of incantation; and the drum beat madly, and the pipe shrilled to a scream, summoning all to issue forth, to leave their peaceful hearths; for a strange rite was preconized in their midst. The streets that were wont to be so still, so hushed with the cool and tranquil veils of darkness, asleep beneath the patronage of the evening star, now danced with glimmering lanterns, resounded with the cries of those who hurried forth, drawn as by a magistral spell; and the songs swelled and triumphed, the reverberant beating of the drum grew louder, and in the midst of the awakened town the players, fantastically arrayed, performed their interlude under the red blaze of torches.

He knew not whether they were players, men that would vanish suddenly as they came, disappearing by the track that climbed the hill; or whether they were indeed magicians, workers of great and efficacious spells, who knew the secret word by which the earth may be transformed into the hall of Gehenna, so that they that gazed and listened, as at a passing spectacle, should be entrapped by the sound and the sight presented to them, should be drawn into the elaborated figures of that mystic dance, and so should be whirled away into those unending mazes on the wild hills that were abhorred, there to wander for evermore.

But Darnell was not afraid, because of the Daystar that had risen in his heart. It had dwelt there all his life, and had slowly shone forth with clearer and clearer light, and he began to see that though his earthly steps might be in the ways of the ancient town that was beset by the Enchanters, and resounded with their songs and their processions, yet he dwelt also in that serene and secure world of brightness, and from a great and unutterable height looked on the confusion of the mortal pageant, beholding mysteries in which he was no true actor, hearing magic songs that could by no means draw him down from the battlements of the high and holy city.

His heart was filled with a great joy and a great peace as he lay down beside his wife and fell asleep, and in the morning, when he woke up, he was glad.

# IV

In a haze as of a dream Darnell's thoughts seemed to move through the opening days of the next week. Perhaps nature had not intended that he should be practical or much given to that which is usually called 'sound common sense,' but his training had made him desirous of good, plain qualities of the mind, and he uneasily strove to account to himself for his strange mood of the Sunday night, as he had often endeavoured to interpret the fancies of his boyhood and early man-hood.

# Arthur Machen

At first he was annoyed by his want of success; the morning paper, which he always secured as the 'bus delayed at Uxbridge Road Station, fell from his hands unread, while he vainly reasoned, assuring himself that the threatened incursion of a whimsical old woman, though tiresome enough, was no rational excuse for those curious hours of meditation in which his thoughts seemed to have dressed themselves in unfamiliar, fantastic habits, and to parley with him in a strange speech, and yet a speech that he had understood.

With such arguments he perplexed his mind on the long, accustomed ride up the steep ascent of Holland Park, past the incongruous hustle of Notting Hill Gate, where in one direction a road shows the way to the snug, somewhat faded bowers and retreats of Bayswater, and in another one sees the portal of the murky region of the slums. The customary companions of his morning's journey were in the seats about him; he heard the hum of their talk, as they disputed concerning politics, and the man next to him, who came from Acton, asked him what he thought of the Government now. There was a discussion, and a loud and excited one, just in front, as to whether rhubarb was a fruit or vegetable, and in his ear he heard Redman, who was a near neighbour, praising the economy of 'the wife.'

'I don't know how she does it. Look here; what do you think we had yesterday? Breakfast: fish-cakes, beautifully fried—rich, you know, lots of herbs, it's a receipt of her aunt's; you should just taste 'em. Coffee, bread, butter, marmalade, and, of course, all the usual etceteras.

Dinner: roast beef, Yorkshire, potatoes, greens, and horse-radish sauce, plum tart, cheese. And where will you get a better dinner than that? Well, I call it wonderful, I really do.'

But in spite of these distractions he fell into a dream as the 'bus rolled and tossed on its way Citywards, and still he strove to solve the enigma of his vigil of the night before, and as the shapes of

84

trees and green lawns and houses passed before his eyes, and as he saw the procession moving on the pavement, and while the murmur of the streets sounded in his ears, all was to him strange and unaccustomed, as if he moved through the avenues of some city in a foreign land. It was, perhaps, on these mornings, as he rode to his mechanical work, that vague and floating fancies that must have long haunted his brain began to shape themselves, and to put on the form of definite conclusions, from which he could no longer escape, even if he had wished it. Darnell had received what is called a sound commercial education, and would therefore have found very great difficulty in putting into articulate speech any thought that was worth thinking; but he grew certain on these mornings that the 'common sense' which he had always heard exalted as man's supremest faculty was, in all probability, the smallest and least-considered item in the equipment of an ant of average intelligence. And with this, as an almost necessary corollary, came a firm belief that the whole fabric of life in which he moved was sunken, past all thinking, in the grossest absurdity; that he and all his friends and acquaintances and fellow-workers were interested in matters in which men were never meant to be interested, were pursuing aims which they were never meant to pursue, were, indeed, much like fair stones of an altar serving as a pigsty wall. Life, it seemed to him, was a great search for—he knew not what; and in the process of the ages one by one the true marks upon the ways had been shattered, or buried, or the meaning of the words had been slowly forgotten; one by one the signs had been turned awry, the true entrances had been thickly overgrown, the very way itself had been diverted from the heights to the depths, till at last the race of pilgrims had become hereditary stone-breakers and ditch-scourers on a track that led to destruction—if it led anywhere at all. Darnell's heart thrilled with a strange and trembling joy, with a sense that was all new, when it came to his mind that this great loss might not be a hopeless one, that perhaps the difficulties were by no means insuperable.

# Arthur Machen

It might be, he considered, that the stonebreaker had merely to throw down his hammer and set out, and the way would be plain before him; and a single step would free the delver in rubbish from the foul slime of the ditch.

It was, of course, with difficulty and slowly that these things became clear to him. He was an English City clerk, 'flourishing' towards the end of the nineteenth century, and the rubbish heap that had been accumulating for some centuries could not be cleared away in an instant. Again and again the spirit of nonsense that had been implanted in him as in his fellows assured him that the true world was the visible and tangible world, the world in which good and faithful letter-copying was exchangeable for a certain quantum of bread, beef, and house-room, and that the man who copied letters well, did not beat his wife, nor lose money foolishly, was a good man, fulfilling the end for which he had been made. But in spite of these arguments, in spite of their acceptance by all who were about him, he had the grace to perceive the utter falsity and absurdity of the whole position. He was fortunate in his entire ignorance of sixpenny 'science,' but if the whole library had been projected into his brain it would not have moved him to 'deny in the darkness that which he had known in the light.' Darnell knew by experience that man is made a mystery for mysteries and visions, for the realization in his consciousness of ineffable bliss, for a great joy that transmutes the whole world, for a joy that surpasses all joys and overcomes all sorrows. He knew this certainly, though he knew it dimly; and he was apart from other men, preparing himself for a great experiment.

With such thoughts as these for his secret and concealed treasure, he was able to bear the threatened invasion of Mrs. Nixon with something approaching indifference. He knew, indeed, that her presence between his wife and himself would be unwelcome to him, and he was not without grave doubts as to the woman's sanity; but after all, what did it matter? Besides, already a faint glimmering light had risen within him that showed the profit of self-negation, and in this matter he had preferred his wife's will to his own. Et non sua pomo; to his astonishment he found a delight in denying himself his own wish, a process that he had always regarded as thoroughly detestable. This was a state of things which he could not in the least understand; but, again, though a member of a most hopeless class, living in the most hopeless surroundings that the world has ever seen, though he knew as much of the askesis as of Chinese metaphysics; again, he had the grace not to deny the light that had begun to glimmer in his soul.

And he found a present reward in the eyes of Mary, when she welcomed him home after his foolish labours in the cool of the evening. They sat together, hand in hand, under the mulberry tree, at the coming of the dusk, and as the ugly walls about them became obscure and vanished into the formless world of shadows, they seemed to be freed from the bondage of Shepherd's Bush, freed to wander in that undisfigured, undefiled world that lies beyond the walls. Of this region Mary knew little or nothing by experience, since her relations had always been of one mind with the modern world, which has for the true country an instinctive and most significant horror and dread. Mr. Reynolds had also shared in another odd superstition of these later days— that it is necessary to leave London at least once a year; consequently Mary had some knowledge of various seaside resorts on the south and east coasts, where Londoners gather in hordes, turn the sands into one vast, bad music-hall, and derive, as they say, enormous benefit from the change. But experiences such as these give but little knowledge of the country in its true and occult sense; and yet Mary, as she sat in the dusk beneath the whispering tree, knew something of the secret of the wood, of the valley shut in by high hills, where the sound of pouring water always echoes from the clear brook. And to Darnell these were nights of great dreams; for it was the hour of the work, the time of transmutation, and he who could not understand the miracle, who could scarcely believe in it, yet knew, secretly and half consciously, that the water was being changed into the wine of a new life. This was ever the inner music of his dreams, and to it he added on these still and sacred nights the far-off memory of that time long ago when, a child, before the world had overwhelmed him, he journeyed down to the old grey house in the west, and for a whole month heard the murmur of the forest through his bedroom window, and when the wind was hushed, the washing of the tides about the reeds; and sometimes awaking very early he had heard the strange cry of a bird as it rose from its nest among the reeds, and had looked out and had seen the valley whiten to the dawn, and the winding river whiten as it swam down to the sea. The memory of all this had faded and become shadowy as he grew older and the chains of common life were riveted firmly about his soul; all the atmosphere by which he was surrounded was well-nigh fatal to such thoughts, and only now and again in half-conscious moments or in sleep he had revisited that valley in the far-off west, where the breath of wind was an incantation, and every leaf and stream and hill spoke of great and ineffable mysteries. But now the broken vision was in great part restored to him, and looking with love in his wife's eyes he saw the gleam of water-pools in the still forest, saw the mists rising in the evening, and heard the music of the winding river.

They were sitting thus together on the Friday evening of the week that had begun with that odd and half-forgotten visit of Mrs. Nixon, when, to Darnell's annoyance, the door-bell gave a discordant peal, and Alice with some disturbance of manner came out and announced that a gentleman wished to see the master. Darnell went into the drawing-room, where Alice had lit one gas so that it flared and burnt with a rushing sound, and in this distorting light there waited a stout, elderly gentleman, whose countenance was altogether unknown to him. He stared blankly, and hesitated, about to speak, but the visitor began.

'You don't know who I am, but I expect you'll know my

name. It's Nixon.' He did not wait to be interrupted. He sat down and plunged into narrative, and after the first few words, Darnell, whose mind was not altogether unprepared, listened without much astonishment.

'And the long and the short of it is,' Mr. Nixon said at last, 'she's gone stark, staring mad, and we had to put her away to-day—poor thing.'

His voice broke a little, and he wiped his eyes hastily, for though stout and successful he was not unfeeling, and he was fond of his wife. He had spoken quickly, and had gone lightly over many details which might have interested specialists in certain kinds of mania, and Darnell was sorry for his evident distress. 'I came here,' he went on after a brief pause, 'because I found out she had been to see you last Sunday, and I knew the sort of story she must have told.'

Darnell showed him the prophetic leaflet which Mrs. Nixon had dropped in the garden. 'Did you know about this?' he said.

'Oh, him,' said the old man, with some approach to cheerfulness; 'oh yes, I thrashed him black and blue the day before yesterday.'

'Isn't he mad? Who is the man?'

'He's not mad, he's bad. He's a little Welsh skunk named Richards. He's been running some sort of chapel over at New Barnet for the last few years, and my poor wife—she never could find the parish church good enough for her—had been going to his damned schism shop for the last twelve-month. It was all that finished her off. Yes; I thrashed him the day before yesterday, and I'm not afraid of a summons either. I know him, and he knows I know him.'

Old Nixon whispered something in Darnell's ear, and chuckled faintly as he repeated for the third time his formula—'I thrashed him black and blue the day before yesterday.'

Darnell could only murmur condolences and express his hope that Mrs. Nixon might recover.

The old man shook his head.

'I'm afraid there's no hope of that,' he said. 'I've had the best advice, but they couldn't do anything, and told me so.'

Presently he asked to see his niece, and Darnell went out and prepared Mary as well as he could. She could scarcely take in the news that her aunt was a hopeless maniac, for Mrs. Nixon, having been extremely stupid all her days, had naturally succeeded in passing with her relations as typically sensible. With the Reynolds family, as with the great majority of us, want of imagination is always equated with sanity, and though many of us have never heard of Lombroso we are his ready-made converts. We have always believed that poets are mad, and if statistics unfortunately show that few poets have really been inhabitants of lunatic asylums, it is soothing to learn that nearly all poets have had whooping-cough, which is doubtless, like intoxication, a minor madness.

'But is it really true?' she asked at length. 'Are you certain uncle is not deceiving you? Aunt seemed so sensible always.'

She was helped at last by recollecting that Aunt Marian used to get up very early of mornings, and then they went into the drawing-room and talked to the old man. His evident kindliness and honesty grew upon Mary, in spite of a lingering belief in her aunt's fables, and when he left, it was with a promise to come to see them again.

Mrs. Darnell said she felt tired, and went to bed; and Darnell returned to the garden and began to pace to and fro, collecting his thoughts. His immeasurable relief at the intelligence that, after all, Mrs. Nixon was not coming to live with them taught him that, despite his submission, his dread of the event had been very great. The weight was removed, and now he was free to consider his life without reference to the grotesque intrusion that he had feared. He sighed for joy, and as he paced to and fro he savoured the scent of the night, which, though it came faintly to him in that brick-bound suburb, summoned to his mind across many years the odour of the world at night as he had known it in that short sojourn of his boyhood; the odour that rose from the earth when the flame of the sun had gone down beyond the mountain, and the afterglow had paled in the sky and on the fields. And as he recovered as best he could these lost dreams of an enchanted land, there came to him other images of his childhood, forgotten and yet not forgotten, dwelling unheeded in dark places of the memory, but ready to be summoned forth. He remembered one fantasy that had long haunted him. As he lay half asleep in the forest on one hot afternoon of that memorable visit to the country, he had 'made believe' that a little companion had come to him out of the blue mists and the green light beneath the leaves—a white girl with long black hair, who had played with him and whispered her secrets in his ear, as his father lay sleeping under a tree; and from that summer afternoon, day by day, she had been beside him; she had visited him in the wilderness of London, and even in recent years there had come to him now and again the sense of her presence, in the midst of the heat and turmoil of the City. The last visit he remembered well; it was a few weeks before he married, and from the depths of some futile task he had looked up with puzzled eyes, wondering why the close air suddenly grew scented with green leaves, why the murmur of the trees and the wash of the river on the reeds came to his ears; and then that sudden rapture to which he had given a name and an individuality possessed him utterly. He knew then how the dull flesh of man can be like fire; and now, looking back from a new standpoint on this and other experiences, he realized how all that was real in his life had been unwelcomed, uncherished by him, had come to him, perhaps, in virtue of merely negative qualities on his part. And yet, as he reflected, he saw that there had been a chain of witnesses all through his life: again and again voices had whispered in his ear words in a strange language that he now recognized as his native tongue; the common street had not been lacking in visions of the true land of his birth; and in all the passing and repassing of the world he saw that there had been emissaries ready to guide his feet on the way of the great journey.

A week or two after the visit of Mr. Nixon, Darnell took his annual holiday.

There was no question of Walton-on-the-Naze, or of anything of the kind, as he quite agreed with his wife's longing for some substantial sum put by against the evil day. But the weather was still fine, and he lounged away the time in his garden beneath the tree, or he sauntered out on long aimless walks in the western purlieus of London, not unvisited by that old sense of some great ineffable beauty, concealed by the dim and dingy veils of grey interminable streets. Once, on a day of heavy rain he went to the 'box-room,' and began to turn over the papers in the old hair trunk—scraps and odds and ends of family history, some of them in his father's handwriting, others in faded ink, and there were a few ancient pocket-books, filled with manuscript of a still earlier time, and in these the ink was glossier and blacker than any writing fluids supplied by stationers of later days. Darnell had hung up the portrait of the ancestor in this room, and had bought a solid kitchen table and a chair; so that Mrs. Darnell, seeing him looking over his old documents, half thought of naming the room 'Mr. Darnell's study.' He had not glanced at these relics of his family for many years, but from the hour when the rainy morning sent him to them, he remained constant to research till the end of the holidays. It was a new interest, and he began to fashion in his mind a faint picture of his forefathers, and of their life in that grey old house in the river valley, in the western land of wells and streams and dark and ancient woods. And there were stranger things than mere notes on family history amongst that odd litter of old disregarded papers, and when he went back to his work in the City some of the men fancied that he was in some vague manner changed in appearance; but he only laughed when they asked him where he had been and what he had been doing with himself. But Mary noticed that every evening he spent at least an hour in the box-room; she was rather sorry at the waste of time involved in reading old papers about dead people. And one afternoon, as they were out together on a somewhat dreary walk towards Acton, Darnell stopped at a hopeless second-hand bookshop, and after scanning the rows of shabby books in the window, went in and purchased two volumes. They proved to be a Latin dictionary and grammar, and she was surprised to hear her husband declare his intention of acquiring the Latin language.

But, indeed, all his conduct impressed her as indefinably altered; and she began to be a little alarmed, though she could scarcely have formed her fears in words. But she knew that in some way that was all indefined and beyond the grasp of her thought their lives had altered since the summer, and no single thing wore quite the same aspect as before. If she looked out into the dull street with its rare loiterers, it was the same and yet it had altered, and if she opened the window in the early morning the wind that entered came with a changed breath that spoke some message that she could not understand. And day by day passed by in the old course, and not even the four walls were altogether familiar, and the voices of men and women sounded with strange notes, with the echo, rather, of a music that came over unknown hills. And day by day as she went about her household work, passing from shop to shop in those dull streets that were a network, a fatal labyrinth of grey desolation on every side, there came to her sense half-seen images of some other world, as if she walked in a dream, and every moment must bring her to light and to awakening, when the grey should fade, and regions long desired should appear in glory. Again and again it seemed as if that which was hidden would be shown even to the sluggish testimony of sense; and as she went to and fro from street to street of that dim and weary suburb, and looked on those grey material walls, they seemed as if a light glowed behind them, and again and again the mystic fragrance of incense was blown to her nostrils from across the verge of that world which is not so much impenetrable as ineffable, and to her ears came the dream of a chant that spoke of hidden choirs about all her ways. She struggled against these impressions, refusing her assent to the testimony of them, since all the pressure of credited opinion for three hundred years has been directed towards stamping out real knowledge, and so effectually has this been accomplished that we can only recover the truth through much anguish. And so Mary passed the days in a strange perturbation, clinging to common things and common thoughts, as if she feared that one morning she would wake up in an unknown world to a changed life. And Edward Darnell went day by day to his labour and returned in the evening, always with that shining of light within his eyes and upon his face, with the gaze of wonder that was greater day by day, as if for him the veil grew thin and soon would disappear.

From these great matters both in herself and in her husband Mary shrank back, afraid, perhaps, that if she began the question the answer might be too wonderful. She rather taught herself to be troubled over little things; she asked herself what attraction there could be in the old records over which she supposed Edward to be poring night after night in the cold room upstairs. She had glanced over the papers at Darnell's invitation, and could see but little interest in them; there were one or two sketches, roughly done in pen and ink, of the old house in the west: it looked a shapeless and fantastic place, furnished with strange pillars and stranger ornaments on the projecting porch; and on one side a roof dipped down almost to the earth, and in the centre there was something that might almost be a tower rising above the rest of the building. Then there were documents that seemed all names and dates, with here and there a coat of arms done in the margin, and she came upon a string of uncouth Welsh names linked together by the word 'ap' in a chain that looked endless. There was a paper covered with signs and figures that meant nothing to her, and then there were the pocket-books, full of old-fashioned writing, and much of it in Latin, as her husband told her—it was a collection as void of significance as a treatise on conic sections, so far as Mary was concerned. But night after night Darnell shut himself up with the musty rolls, and more than ever when he rejoined her he bore upon his face the blazonry of some great adventure. And one night she asked him what interested him so much in the papers he had shown her.

He was delighted with the question. Somehow they had not talked much together for the last few weeks, and he began to tell her of the records of the old race from which he came, of the old strange house of grey stone between the forest and the river. The family went back and back, he said, far into the dim past, beyond the Normans, beyond the Saxons, far into the Roman days, and for many hundred years they had been petty kings, with a strong fortress high up on the hill, in the heart of the forest; and even now the great mounds remained, whence one could look through the trees towards the mountain on one side and across the yellow sea on the other. The real name of the family was not Darnell; that was assumed by one Iolo ap Taliesin ap Iorwerth in the sixteenth century—why, Darnell did not seem to understand. And then he told her how the race had dwindled in prosperity, century by century, till at last there was nothing left but the grey house and a few acres of land bordering the river.

'And do you know, Mary,' he said, 'I suppose we shall go and live there some day or other.

'My great-uncle, who has the place now, made money in business when he was a young man, and I believe he will leave it all to me. I know I am the only relation he has. How strange it would be.

'What a change from the life here.'

'You never told me that. Don't you think your great-uncle

might leave his house and his money to somebody he knows really well? You haven't seen him since you were a little boy, have you?'

'No; but we write once a year. And from what I have heard my father say, I am sure the old man would never leave the house out of the family. Do you think you would like it?'

'I don't know. Isn't it very lonely?'

'I suppose it is. I forget whether there are any other houses in sight, but I don't think there are any at all near. But what a change! No City, no streets, no people passing to and fro; only the sound of the wind and the sight of the green leaves and the green hills, and the song of the voices of the earth.' . . . . He checked himself suddenly, as if he feared that he was about to tell some secret that must not yet be uttered; and indeed, as he spoke of the change from the little street in Shepherd's Bush to that ancient house in the woods of the far west, a change seemed already to possess himself, and his voice put on the modulation of an antique chant. Mary looked at him steadily and touched his arm, and he drew a long breath before he spoke again.

'It is the old blood calling to the old land,' he said. 'I was forgetting that I am a clerk in the City.'

It was, doubtless, the old blood that had suddenly stirred in him; the resurrection of the old spirit that for many centuries had been faithful to secrets that are now disregarded by most of us, that now day by day was quickened more and more in his heart, and grew so strong that it was hard to conceal. He was indeed almost in the position of the man in the tale, who, by a sudden electric shock, lost the vision of the things about him in the London streets, and gazed instead upon the sea and shore of an island in the Antipodes; for Darnell only clung with an effort to the interests and the atmosphere which, till lately, had seemed all the world to him; and the grey house and the wood and the river, symbols of the other sphere, intruded as it were into the landscape of the London suburb.

But he went on, with more restraint, telling his stories of far-off ancestors, how one of them, the most remote of all, was called a saint, and was supposed to possess certain mysterious secrets often alluded to in the papers as the 'Hidden Songs of Iolo Sant.' And then with an abrupt transition he recalled memories of his father and of the strange, shiftless life in dingy lodgings in the backwaters of London, of the dim stucco streets that were his first recollections, of forgotten squares in North London, and of the figure of his father, a grave bearded man who seemed always in a dream, as if he too sought for the vision of a land beyond the strong walls, a land where there were deep orchards and many shining hills, and fountains and water-pools gleaming under the leaves of the wood.

'I believe my father earned his living,' he went on, 'such a living as he did earn, at the Record Office and the British Museum. He used to hunt up things for lawyers and country parsons who wanted old deeds inspected. He never made much, and we were always moving from one lodging to another—always to out-of-the-way places where everything seemed to have run to seed. We never knew our neighbours—we moved too often for that—but my father had about half a dozen friends, elderly men like himself, who used to come to see us pretty often; and then, if there was any money, the lodging-house servant would go out for beer, and they would sit and smoke far into the night.

'I never knew much about these friends of his, but they all had the same look, the look of longing for something hidden. They talked of mysteries that I never understood, very little of their own lives, and when they did speak of ordinary affairs one could tell that they thought such matters as money and the want of it were unimportant trifles. When I grew up and went into the City, and met other young fellows and heard their way of talking, I wondered whether my father and his friends were not a little queer in their heads; but I know better now.'

So night after night Darnell talked to his wife, seeming to wander aimlessly from the dingy lodging-houses, where he had spent his boyhood in the company of his father and the other seekers, to the old house hidden in that far western valley, and the old race that had so long looked at the setting of the sun over the mountain. But in truth there was one end in all that he spoke, and Mary felt that beneath his words, however indifferent they might seem, there was hidden a purpose, that they were to embank on a great and marvellous adventure.

So day by day the world became more magical; day by day the work of separation was being performed, the gross accidents were being refined away. Darnell neglected no instruments that might be useful in the work; and now he neither lounged at home on Sunday mornings, nor did he accompany his wife to the Gothic blasphemy which pretended to be a church. They had discovered a little church of another fashion in a back street, and Darnell, who had found in one of the old notebooks the maxim Incredibilia sola Credenda, soon perceived how high and glorious a thing was that service at which he assisted. Our stupid ancestors taught us that we could become wise by studying books on 'science,' by meddling with test-tubes, geological specimens, microscopic preparations, and the like; but they who have cast off these follies know that they must read not 'science' books, but mass-books, and that the soul is made wise by the contemplation of mystic ceremonies and elaborate and curious rites. In such things Darnell found a wonderful mystery language, which spoke at once more secretly and more directly than the formal creeds; and he saw that, in a sense, the whole world is but a great ceremony or sacrament, which teaches under visible forms a hidden and transcendent doctrine. It was thus that he found in the ritual of the church a perfect image of the world; an image purged, exalted, and illuminate, a holy house built up of shining and translucent stones, in which the burning torches were more significant than the wheeling stars, and the fuming incense was a more certain token than the rising of the mist. His soul went forth with the albed procession in its white and solemn order, the mystic dance that signifies rapture and a joy above all joys, and when he beheld Love slain and rise again victorious he knew that he witnessed, in a figure, the consummation of all things, the Bridal of all Bridals, the mystery that is beyond all mysteries, accomplished from the foundation of the world. So day by day the house of his life became more magical.

And at the same time he began to guess that if in the New Life there are new and unheard-of joys, there are also new and unheard-of dangers. In his manuscript books which professed to deliver the outer sense of those mysterious 'Hidden Songs of Iolo Sant' there was a little chapter that bore the heading: Fons Sacer non in communem Vsum convertendus est, and by diligence, with much use of the grammar and dictionary, Darnell was able to construe the by no means complex Latin of his ancestor. The special book which contained the chapter in question was one of the most singular in the collection, since it bore the title Terra de Iolo, and on the surface, with an ingenious concealment of its real symbolism, it affected to give an account of the orchards, fields, woods, roads, tenements, and waterways in the possession of Darnell's ancestors. Here, then, he read of the Holy Well, hidden in the Wistman's Wood—Sylva Sapientum—'a fountain of abundant water, which no heats of summer can ever dry, which no flood can ever defile, which is as a water of life, to them that thirst for life, a stream of cleansing to them that would be pure, and a medicine of such healing virtue that by it, through the might of God and the intercession of His saints, the most grievous wounds are made whole.'

But the water of this well was to be kept sacred perpetually, it was not to be used for any common purpose, nor to satisfy any bodily thirst; but ever to be esteemed as holy, 'even as the water which the priest hath hallowed.' And in the margin a comment in a later hand taught Darnell something of the meaning of these prohibitions. He was warned not to use the Well of Life as a mere luxury of mortal life, as a new sensation, as a means of making the insipid cup of everyday existence more palatable. 'For,' said the commentator, 'we are not called to sit as the spectators in a theatre, there to watch the play performed before us, but we are rather summoned to stand in the very scene itself, and there fervently to enact our parts in a great and wonderful mystery.'

Darnell could quite understand the temptation that was thus indicated. Though he had gone but a little way on the path, and had barely tested the over-runnings of that mystic well, he was already aware of the enchantment that was transmuting all the world about him, informing his life with a strange significance and romance. London seemed a city of the Arabian Nights, and its labyrinths of streets an enchanted maze; its long avenues of lighted lamps were as starry systems, and its immensity became for him an image of the endless universe. He could well imagine how pleasant it might be to linger in such a world as this, to sit apart and dream, beholding the strange pageant played before him; but the Sacred Well was not for common use, it was for the cleansing of the soul, and the healing of the grievous wounds of the spirit. There must be yet another transformation: London had become Bagdad; it must at last be transmuted to Syon, or in the phrase of one of his old documents, the City of the Cup.

And there were yet darker perils which the Iolo MSS. (as his father had named the collection) hinted at more or less obscurely. There were suggestions of an awful region which the soul might enter, of a transmutation that was unto death, of evocations which could summon the utmost forces of evil from their dark places—in a word, of that sphere which is represented to most of us under the crude and somewhat childish symbolism of Black Magic. And here again he was not altogether without a dim comprehension of what was meant. He found himself recalling an odd incident that had happened long ago, which had remained all the years in his mind unheeded, amongst the many insignificant recollections of his childhood, and now rose before him, clear and distinct and full of meaning. It was on that memorable visit to the old house in the west, and the whole scene returned, with its smallest events, and the voices seemed to sound in his ears. It was a grey, still day of heavy heat that he remembered: he had stood on the lawn after breakfast, and wondered at the great peace and silence of the world. Not a leaf stirred in the trees on the lawn, not a whisper came from the myriad leaves of the wood; the flowers gave out sweet and heavy odours as if they breathed the dreams of the summer night; and far down the valley, the winding river was like dim silver under that dim and silvery sky, and the far hills and woods and fields vanished in the mist. The stillness of the air held him as with a charm; he leant all the morning against the rails that parted the lawn from the meadow, breathing the mystic breath of summer, and watching the fields brighten as with a sudden blossoming of shining flowers as the high mist grew thin for a moment before the hidden sun. As he watched thus, a man weary with heat, with some glance of horror in his eyes, passed him on his way to the house; but he stayed at his post till the old bell in the turret rang, and they dined all together, masters and servants, in the dark cool room that looked towards the still leaves of the wood. He could see that his uncle was upset about something, and when they had finished dinner he heard him tell his father that there was trouble at a farm; and it was settled that they should all drive over in the afternoon to some place with a strange name. But when the time came Mr. Darnell was too deep in old books and tobacco smoke to be stirred from his corner, and Edward and his uncle went alone in the dog-cart.

They drove swiftly down the narrow lane, into the road that followed the winding river, and crossed the bridge at Caermaen by the mouldering Roman walls, and then, skirting the deserted, echoing village, they came out on a broad white turnpike road, and the limestone dust followed them like a cloud. Then, suddenly, they turned to the north by such a road as Edward had never seen before. It was so narrow that there was barely room for the cart to pass, and the footway was of rock, and the banks rose high above them as they slowly climbed the long, steep way, and the untrimmed hedges on either side shut out the light. And the ferns grew thick and green upon the banks, and hidden wells dripped down upon them; and the old man told him how the lane in winter was a torrent of swirling water, so that no one could pass by it. On they went, ascending and then again descending, always in that deep hollow under the wild woven boughs, and the boy wondered vainly what the country was like on either side. And now the air grew darker, and the hedge on one bank was but the verge of a dark and rustling wood, and the grey limestone rocks had changed to dark-red earth flecked with green patches and veins of marl, and suddenly in the stillness from the depths of the wood a bird began to sing a melody that charmed the heart into another world, that sang to the child's soul of the blessed faery realm beyond the woods of the earth, where the wounds of man are healed. And so at last, after many turnings and windings, they came to a high bare land where the lane broadened out into a kind of common, and along the edge of this place there were scattered three or four old cottages, and one of them was a little tavern. Here they stopped, and a man came out and tethered the tired horse to a post and gave him water; and old Mr. Darnell took the child's hand and led him by a path across the fields. The boy could see the country now, but it was all a strange, undiscovered land; they were in the heart of a wilderness of hills and valleys that he had never looked upon, and they were going down a wild, steep hillside, where the narrow path wound in and out amidst gorse and towering bracken, and the sun gleaming out for a moment, there was a gleam of white water far below in a narrow valley, where a little brook poured and rippled from stone to stone. They went down the hill, and through a brake, and then, hidden in dark-green orchards, they came upon a long, low whitewashed house, with a stone roof strangely coloured by the growth of moss and lichens. Mr. Darnell knocked at a heavy oaken door, and they came into a dim room where but little light entered through the thick glass in the deep-set window. There were heavy beams in the ceiling, and a great fire-place sent out an odour of burning wood that Darnell never forgot, and the room seemed to him full of women who talked all together in frightened tones. Mr. Darnell beckoned to a tall, grey old man, who wore corduroy knee-breeches, and the boy, sitting on a high straight-backed chair, could see the old man and his uncle passing to and fro across the window-panes, as they walked together on the garden path. The women stopped their talk for a moment, and one of them brought him a glass of milk and an apple from some cold inner chamber; and then, suddenly, from a room above there rang out a shrill and terrible shriek, and then, in a young girl's voice, a more terrible song. It was not like anything the child had ever heard, but as the man recalled it to his memory, he knew to what song it might be compared—to a certain chant indeed that summons the angels and archangels to assist in the great Sacrifice. But as this song chants of the heavenly army, so did that seem to summon all the hierarchy of evil, the hosts of Lilith and Samael; and the words that rang out with such awful modulations—neumata inferorum—were in some unknown tongue that few men have even heard on earth.

The women glared at one another with horror in their eyes, and he saw one or two of the oldest of them clumsily making an old sign upon their breasts. Then they began to speak again, and he remembered fragments of their talk.

'She has been up there,' said one, pointing vaguely oven her shoulder.

'She'd never know the way,' answered another. 'They be all gone that went there.'

'There be nought there in these days.'

'How can you tell that, Gwenllian? 'Tis not for us to say that.'

'My great-grandmother did know some that had been there,' said a very old woman. 'She told me how they was taken afterwards.'

And then his uncle appeared at the door, and they went their way as they had come. Edward Darnell never heard any more of it, nor whether the girl died or recovered from her strange attack; but the scene had haunted his mind in boyhood, and now the recollection of it came to him with a certain note of warning, as a symbol of dangers that might be in the way.

It would be impossible to carry on the history of Edward Darnell and of Mary his wife to a greater length, since from this point their legend is full of impossible events, and seems to put on the semblance of the stories of the Graal. It is certain, indeed, that in this world they changed their lives, like King Arthur, but this is a work which no chronicler has cared to describe with any amplitude of detail. Darnell, it is true, made a little book, partly consisting of queer verse which might have been written by an inspired infant, and partly made up of 'notes and exclamations' in an odd dog-Latin which he had picked up from the 'Iolo MSS.', but it is to be feared that this work, even if published in its entirety, would cast but little light on a perplexing story. He called this piece of literature 'In Exitu Israel,' and wrote on the title page the motto, doubtless of his own composition, 'Nunc certe scio quod omnia legenda; omnes historiæ, omnes fabulæ, omnis Scriptura sint de ME narrata.' It is only too evident that his Latin was not learnt at the feet of Cicero; but in this dialect he relates the great history of the 'New Life' as it was manifested to him. The 'poems' are even stranger. One, headed (with an odd reminiscence of old-fashioned books) 'Lines written on looking down from a Height in London on a Board School suddenly lit up by the Sun' begins thus:—

One day when I was all alone
I found a wondrous little stone,

## A Fragment of Life

It lay forgotten on the road
Far from the ways of man's abode.
When on this stone mine eyes I cast
I saw my Treasure found at last.
I pressed it hard against my face,
I covered it with my embrace,
I hid it in a secret place.
And every day I went to see
This stone that was my ecstasy;
And worshipped it with flowers rare,
And secret words and sayings fair.
O stone, so rare and red and wise
O fragment of far Paradise,
O Star, whose light is life!
O Sea, Whose ocean is infinity!
Thou art a fire that ever burns,
And all the world to wonder turns;
And all the dust of the dull day
By thee is changed and purged away,
So that, where'er I look, I see
A world of a Great Majesty.
The sullen river rolls all gold,
The desert park's a faery wold,
When on the trees the wind is borne
I hear the sound of Arthur's horn
I see no town of grim grey ways,
But a great city all ablaze
With burning torches, to light up
The pinnacles that shrine the Cup.
Ever the magic wine is poured,
Ever the Feast shines on the board,
Ever the song is borne on high
That chants the holy Magistry—

Etc. etc. etc. From such documents as these it is clearly impossible to gather any very definite information.

But on the last page Darnell has written— 'So I awoke from a dream of a London suburb, of daily labour, of weary, useless little things; and as my eyes were opened I saw that I was in an ancient wood, where a clear well rose into grey film and vapour beneath a misty, glimmering heat. And a form came towards me from the hidden places of the wood, and my love and I were united by the well.'

THE END

# THE CHILDREN
# OF THE POOL

A couple of summers ago I was staying with old friends in my native county, on the Welsh border. It was in the heat and drought of a hot and dry year, and I came into those green, well-watered valleys with a sense of a great refreshment. Here was relief from the burning of London streets, from the close and airless nights, when all the myriad walls of brick and stone and concrete and the pavements that are endless give out into the heavy darkness the fires that all day long have been drawn from the sun. And from those roadways that have become like railways, with their changing lamps, and their yellow globes, and their bars and studs of steel; from the menace of instant death if your feet stray from the track: from all this what a rest to walk under the green leaf in quiet, and hear the stream trickling from the heart of the hill.

My friends were old friends, and they were urgent that I should go my own way. There was breakfast at nine, but it was equally serviceable and excellent at ten; and I could be in for something cold for lunch, if I liked; and if I didn't like I could stay away till dinner at half past seven; and then there was all the evening for talks about old times and about the changes, with comfortable drinks, and bed soothed by memories and tobacco, and by the brook that twisted under dark alders through the meadow below. And not a red bungalow to be seen for many a mile around! Sometimes, when the heat even in that green land was more than burning, and the wind from the mountains in the west ceased, I would stay all day under shade on the lawn, but more often I went afield and trod remembered ways, and tried to find new ones, in that happy and bewildered country. There, paths go wandering into undiscovered valleys, there from deep and narrow lanes with overshadowing hedges, still smaller tracks that I suppose are old bridlepaths, creep obscurely, obviously leading nowhere in particular.

It was on a day of cooler air that I went adventuring abroad on such an expedition. It was a "day of the veil." There were no clouds in the sky, but a high mist, grey and luminous, had been drawn all over it. At one moment, it would seem that the sun must shine through, and the blue appear; and then the trees in the wood would seem to blossom, and the meadows lightened; and then again the veil would be drawn. I struck off by the stony lane that led from the back of the house up over the hill; I had last gone that way a-many years ago, of a winter afternoon, when the ruts were frozen into hard ridges, and dark pines on high places rose above snow, and the sun was red and still above the mountain. I remembered that the way had given good sport, with twists to right and left, and unexpected descents, and then risings to places of thorn and bracken, till it darkened to the hushed stillness of a winter's night, and I turned homeward reluctant. Now I took another chance with all the summer day before me, and resolved to come to some end and conclusion of the matter.

I think I had gone beyond the point at which I had stopped and turned back as the frozen darkness and the bright stars came on me. I remembered the dip in the hedge, from which I saw the round tumulus on high at the end of the mountain wall; and there was the white farm on the hill-side, and the farmer was still calling to his dog, as he—or his father—had called before, his voice high and thin in the distance. After this point, I seemed to be in undis-covered country; the ash trees grew densely on either side of the way and met above it: I went on and on into the unknown in the manner of the only good guide-books, which are the tales of old knights. The road went down, and climbed, and again descended, all through the deep of the wood. Then, on both sides, the trees ceased, though the hedges were so high that I could see nothing of the way of the land about me. And just at the wood's ending, there was one of those tracks or little paths of which I have spoken, going off from my lane on the right, and winding out of sight quickly under all its leafage of hazel and wild rose, maple and hornbeam, with a holly here and there, and honeysuckle golden, and dark briony shining and twining everywhere. I could not resist the invitation of a path so obscure and uncertain, and set out on its track of green and profuse grass, with the ground beneath still soft to the feet, even in the drought of that fiery summer. The way wound, as far as I could make out, on the slope of a hill, neither ascending nor descending, and after a mile or more of this rich walking, it suddenly ceased, and I found myself on a bare hill-side, on a rough track that went down to a grey house. It was now a farm by its looks and surroundings, but there were signs of old state about it: good sixteenth-century mullioned windows and a Jacobean porch projecting from the centre, with dim armorial bearings mouldering above the door.

It struck me that bread and cheese and cider would be grateful, and I beat upon the door with my stick, and brought a pleasant woman to open it.

"Do you think," I began, "you could be so good as...."

And then came a shout from somewhere at the end of the stone passage, and a great voice called:

"Come in, then, come in, you old scoundrel, if your name is Meyrick, as I'm sure it is."

I was amazed. The pleasant woman grinned and said:

"It seems you are well known here, sir, already. But perhaps you had heard that Mr. Roberts was staying here."

My old acquaintance, James Roberts, came tumbling out from his den at the back. He was a man whom I had known a long time, but not very well. Our affairs in London moved on different lines, and so we did not often meet. But I was glad to see him in that unexpected place: he was a round man, always florid and growing redder in the face with his years. He was a countryman of mine, but I had hardly known him before we both went to town, since his home had been at the northern end of the county.

He shook me cordially by the hand, and looked as if he would like to smack me on the back—he was, a little, that kind of man—and repeated his "Come in, come in!" adding to the pleasant woman:

"And bring you another plate, Mrs. Morgan, and all the rest of it. I hope you've not forgotten how to eat Caerphilly cheese, Meyrick. I can tell you, there is none better than Mrs. Morgan's making. And, Mrs. Morgan, another jug of cider, and *seidr dda*, mind you."

I never knew whether he had been brought up as a boy to speak Welsh. In London he had lost all but the faintest trace of accent, but down here in Gwent the tones of the country had quickly returned to him; and he smacked as strongly of the land in his speech as the cheerful farmer's wife herself. I judged his accent was a part of his holiday.

He drew me into the little parlour with its old furniture and its pleasant old-fashioned ornaments and faintly flowering wallpaper, and set me in an elbow-chair at the round table, and gave me, as I told him, exactly what I had meant to ask for; bread and cheese and cider. All very good; Mrs. Morgan, it was clear, had the art of making a Caerphilly cheese that was succulent—a sort of white *bel paese*—far different from those dry and stony cheeses that often bring dishonour on the Caerphilly name. And afterwards there was gooseberry jam and cream. And the tobacco that the country uses: Shag-on-the-Back, from the Welsh Back, Bristol. And then there was gin.

This last we partook of out of doors, in an old stone summerhouse, in the garden at the side. A white rose had grown all over the summer-house, and shaded and glorified it. The water in the big jug had just been drawn from the well in the limestone rock—and I told Roberts gratefully that I felt a great deal better than when I had knocked at the farmhouse door. I told him where I was staying—he knew my host by name—and he, in turn, informed me that it was his first visit to Lanypwll, as the farm was called. A neighbour of his at Lee had recommended Mrs. Morgan's cooking very highly: and, as he said, you couldn't speak too well of her in that way or any other.

We sipped and smoked through the afternoon in that pleasant retreat under the white roses, I meditated gratefully on the fact that I should not dare to enjoy Shag-on-the-Back so freely in London: a potent tobacco, of full and ripe savour, but not for the hard streets,

"You say the farm is called Lanypwll," I interjected, "that means 'by the pool,' doesn't it? Where is the pool? I don't see it."

"Come you," said Roberts, "and I will show you."

He took me by a little gate through the garden hedge of laurels, thick and high, and round to the left of the house, the opposite side to that by which I had made my approach. And there we climbed a green rounded bastion of the old ages, and he pointed down to a narrow valley, shut in by steep wooded hills. There at the bottom was a level, half marshland and half black water lying in still pools, with green islands of iris and of all manner of rank and strange growths that love to have their roots in slime.

"There is your pool for you," said Roberts.

It was the most strange place. I thought, hidden away under the hills as if it were a secret. The steeps that went down to it were a tangle of undergrowth, of all manner of boughs mingled with taller trees rising above the mass, and down at the edge of the marsh some of these had perished in the swampy water, and stood white and bare and ghastly, with leprous limbs.

"An ugly looking place," I said to Roberts.

"I quite agree with you. It is an ugly place enough. They tell me at the farm it's not safe to go near it, or you may get fever and I don't know what else. And, indeed, if you didn't go down carefully and watch your steps, you might easily find yourself up to the neck in that black muck there."

We turned back into the garden and to our summer-house, and soon after, it was time for me to make my way home.

"How long are you staying with Nichol?" Roberts asked me as we parted. I told him, and he insisted on my dining with him at the end of the week.

"I will 'send' you," he said. "I will take you by a short cut across the fields and see that you don't lose your way. Roast duck and green peas," he added alluringly, "and something good for the digestion afterwards."

It was a fine evening when I next journeyed to the farm, but indeed we got tired of saying "fine weathers" throughout that wonderful summer. I found Roberts cheery and welcoming, but, I thought, hardly in such rosy spirits as on my former visit. We were having a cocktail of his composition in the summer-house, as the famous duck gained the last glow of brown perfection; and I noticed that his speech was not bubbling so freely from him as before. He fell silent once or twice and looked thoughtful. He told me he'd ventured down to the pool, the swampy place at the bottom. "And it looks no better when you see it close at hand. Black, oily stuff that isn't like water, with a scum upon it, and weeds like a lot of monsters. I never saw such queer, ugly plants. There's one rank-looking thing down there covered with dull crimson blossoms, all bloated out and speckled like a toad."

"You're no botanist," I remarked.

"No, not I. I know buttercups and daisies and not much more. Mrs. Morgan here was quite frightened when I told her where I'd been. She said she hoped I mightn't be sorry for it. But I feel as well as ever. I don't think there are many places left in the country now where you can get malaria."

We proceeded to the duck and the green peas and rejoiced in their perfection. There was some very old ale that Mr. Morgan had bought when an ancient tavern in the neighbourhood had been pulled down; its age and original excellence had combined to make a drink like a rare wine. The "something good for the digestion" turned out to be a mellow brandy that Roberts had brought with him from town. I told him that I had never known a better hour. He warmed up with the good meat and drink and was cheery enough; and yet I thought there was a reserve, something obscure at the back of his mind that was by no means cheerful.

We had a second glass of the mellow brandy, and Roberts, after a moment's indecision, spoke out. He dropped his holiday game of Welsh countryman completely.

"You wouldn't think, would you." he began, "that a man would come down to a place like this to be blackmailed at the end of the journey?"

"Good Lord!" I gasped in amazement, "I should think not indeed. What's happened?"

He looked very grave. I thought even that he looked frightened.

"Well, I'll tell you. A couple of nights ago, I went for a stroll after my dinner; a beautiful night, with the moon shining, and a nice, clean breeze. So I walked up over the hill, and then took the path that leads down through the wood to the brook. I'd got into the wood, fifty yards or so, when I heard my name called out: 'Roberts! James Roberts!' in a shrill, piercing voice, a young girl's voice, and I jumped pretty well out of my skin, I can tell you. I stopped dead and stared all about me. Of course I could see nothing at all—bright moonlight and black shadow and all those trees—anybody could hide. Then it came to me that it was some girl of the place having a game with her sweetheart: James Roberts is a common enough name, especially in this part of the country. So I was just going on, not bothering my head about the local love-affairs, when that scream came right in my ear: 'Roberts! Roberts! James Roberts!'—and then half a dozen words that I won't trouble you with; not yet, at any rate."

I have said that Roberts was by no means an intimate

friend of mine. But I had always known him as a genial, cordial fellow, a thoroughly good-natured man; and I was sorry and shocked, too, to see him sitting there wretched and dismayed. He looked as if he had seen a ghost; he looked much worse than that. He looked as if he had seen terror.

But it was too early to press him closely. I said:

"What did you do then?"

"I turned about, and ran back through the wood, and tumbled over the stile. I got home here as quick as ever I could, and shut myself up in this room, dripping with fright and gasping for breath. I was almost crazy, I believe. I walked up and down. I sat down in the chair and got up again. I wondered whether I should wake up in my bed and find I'd been having a nightmare. I cried at last; I'll tell you the truth: I put my head in my hands, and the tears ran down my cheeks. I was quite broken."

"But, look here," I said, "isn't this making a great to-do about very little? I can quite see it must have been a nasty shock. But, how long did you say you had been staying here; ten days, was it?"

"A fortnight, to-morrow."

"Well; you know country ways as well as I do. You may be sure that everybody within three or four miles of Lanypwll knows about a gentleman from London, a Mr. James Roberts, staying at the farm. And there are always unpleasant young people to be found, wherever you go. I gather that this girl used very abusive language when she hailed you. She probably thought it was a good joke. You had taken that walk through the wood in the evening a couple of times before? No doubt, you had been noticed going that way, and the girl and her friend or friends planned to give you a shock. I wouldn't think any more of it, if I were you."

He almost cried out.

"Think any more of it! What will the world think of it?" There was an anguish of terror in his voice. I thought it was time to come to cues. I spoke up pretty briskly:

116

"Now, look here, Roberts, it's no good beating about the bush. Before we can do anything, we've got to have the whole tale, fair and square. What I've gathered is this: you go for a walk in a wood near here one evening, and a girl—you say it was a girl's voice—hails you by your name, and then screams out a lot of filthy language. Is there anything more in it than that?"

"There's a lot more than that. I was going to ask you not to let it go any further; but as far as I can see, there won't be any secret in it much longer. There's another end to the story, and it goes back a good many years—to the time when I first came to London as a young man. That's twenty-five years ago."

He stopped speaking. When he began again, I could feel that he spoke with unutterable repugnance. Every word was a horror to him.

"You know as well as I do, that there are all sorts of turnings in London that a young fellow can take; good, bad, and indifferent. There was a good deal of bad luck about it. I do believe, and I was too young to know or care much where I was going; but I got into a turning with the black pit at the end of it."

He beckoned me to lean forward across the table, and whispered for a minute or two in my ear. In my turn, I heard not without horror. I said nothing.

"That was what I heard shrieked out in the wood. What do you say?"

"You've done with all that long ago?"

"It was done with very soon after it was begun. It was no more than a bad dream. And then it all flashed back on me like deadly lightning. What do you say? What can I do?"

I told him that I had to admit that it was no good to try to put the business in the wood down to accident, the casual filthy language of a depraved village girl. As I said, it couldn't be a case of a bow drawn at a venture.

"There must be somebody behind it. Can you think of anybody?"

"There may be one or two left. I can't say. I haven't heard of any of them for years. I thought they had all gone; dead, or at the other side of the world."

"Yes; but people can get back from the other side of the world pretty quickly in these days. Yokohama is not much farther off than Yarmouth. But you haven't heard of any of these people lately?"

"As I said, not for years. But the secret's out."

"But, let's consider. Who is this girl? Where does she live? We must get at her, and try if we can't frighten the life out of her. And, in the first place, we'll find out the source of her information. Then we shall know where we are. I suppose you have discovered who she is?"

"I've not a notion of who she is or where she lives."

"I daresay you wouldn't care to ask the Morgans any questions. But to go back to the beginning: you spoke of blackmail. Did this damned girl ask you for money to shut her mouth?"

"No; I shouldn't have called it blackmail. She didn't say anything about money."

"Well; that sounds more helpful. Let's see; to-night is Saturday. You took this unfortunate walk of yours a couple of nights ago; on Thursday night. And you haven't heard anything more since. I should keep away from that wood, and try to find out who the young lady is. That's the first thing to be done, clearly."

I was trying to cheer him up a little; but he only stared at me with his horror-stricken eyes.

"It didn't finish with the wood," he groaned. "My bedroom is next door to this room where we are. When I had pulled myself together a bit that night, I had a stiff glass, about double my allowance, and went off to bed and to sleep. I woke up with a noise of tapping at the window, just by the head of the bed. Tap, tap, tap, it went. I thought it might be a bough beating on the glass. And then I heard that voice calling me: 'James Roberts: open, open!'

"I tell you, my flesh crawled on my bones. I would have

cried out, but I couldn't make a sound. The moon had gone down, and there's a great old pear tree close to the window, and it was quite dark. I sat up in my bed, shaking for fear. It was dead still, and I began to think that the fright I had got in the wood had given me a nightmare. Then the voice called again, and louder:

"'James Roberts! Open. Quick.'

"And I had to open. I leaned half out of bed, and got at the latch, and opened the window a little. I didn't dare to look out. But it was too dark to see anything in the shadow of the tree. And then she began to talk to me. She told me all about it from the beginning. She knew all the names. She knew where my business was in London, and where I lived, and who my friends were. She said that they should all know. And she said: 'And you yourself shall tell them, and you shall not be able to keep back a single word!'"

The wretched man fell back in his chair, shuddering and gasping for breath. He beat his hands up and down, with a gesture of hopeless fear and misery; and his lips grinned with dread.

I won't say that I began to see light. But I saw a hint of certain possibilities of light or—let us say—of a lessening of the darkness. I said a soothing word or two, and let him get a little quieter. The telling of this extraordinary and very dreadful experience had set his nerves all dancing; and yet, having made a clean breast of it all, I could see that he felt some relief. His hands lay quiet on the table, and his lips ceased their horrible grimacing. He looked at me with a faint expectancy, I thought; as if he had begun to cherish a dim hope that I might have some sort of help for him. He could not see himself the possibility of rescue; still, one never knew what resources and freedoms the other man might bring.

That, at least, was what his poor, miserable face seemed to me to express; and I hoped I was right, and let him simmer a little, and gather to himself such twigs and straws of hope as he could. Then, I began again:

"This was on the Thursday night. And last night? Another visit?"

"The same as before. Almost word for word."

"And it was all true, what she said? The girl was not lying?"

"Every word of it was true. There were some things that I had forgotten myself; but when she spoke of them, I remembered at once. There was the number of a house in a certain street, for example. If you had asked me for that number a week ago I should have told you, quite honestly, that I knew nothing about it. But when I heard it, I knew it in the instant: I could see that number in the light of a street lamp. The sky was dark and cloudy, and a bitter wind was blowing, and driving the leaves on the pavement—that November night."

"When the fire was lit?"

"That night. When they appeared."

"And you haven't seen this girl? You couldn't describe her?"

"I was afraid to look; I told you. I waited when she stopped speaking. I sat there for half an hour or an hour. Then I lit my candle and shut the window-latch. It was three o'clock and growing light."

I was thinking it over. I noted, that Roberts confessed that every word spoken by his visitant was true. She had sprung no surprises on him; there had been no suggestion of fresh details, names, or circumstances. That struck me as having a certain—possible—significance; and the knowledge of Roberts's present circumstances, his City address, and his home address, and the names of his friends: that was interesting, too.

There was a glimpse of a possible hypothesis. I could not be sure; but I told Roberts that I thought something might be done. To begin with, I said, I was going to keep him company for the night. Nichol would guess that I had shirked the walk home after nightfall; that would be quite all right. And in the morning he was to pay Mrs. Morgan for the two extra weeks he had arranged to stay, with something by way of compensation. "And it should be something handsome," I added with emotion, thinking of the duck and the old ale. "And then," I finished, "I shall pack you off to the other side of the island."

Of that old ale I made him drink a liberal dose by way of sleeping-draught. He hardly needed a hypnotic; the terror that he had endured and the stress of telling it had worn him out. I saw him fall into bed and fall asleep in a moment, and I curled up, comfortably enough, in a roomy armchair. There was no trouble in the night, and when I writhed myself awake, I saw Roberts sleeping peacefully. I let him alone, and wandered about the house and the shining morning garden, till I came upon Mrs. Morgan, busy in the kitchen.

I broke the trouble to her. I told her that I was afraid that the place was not agreeing at all with Mr. Roberts. "Indeed," I said, "he was taken so ill last night that I was afraid to leave him. His nerves seem to be in a very bad way."

"Indeed, then, I don't wonder at all," replied Mrs. Morgan, with a very grave face. But I wondered a good deal at this remark of hers, not having a notion as to what she meant.

I went on to explain what I had arranged for our patient, as I called him: east-coast breezes, and crowds of people, the noisier the better, and, indeed, that was the cure that I had in mind. I said that I was sure Mr. Roberts would do the proper thing.

"That will be all right, sir, I am sure: don't you trouble yourself about that. But the sooner you get him away after I have given you both your breakfasts, the better I shall be pleased. I am frightened to death for him, I can tell you."

And she went off to her work, murmuring something that sounded like "*Plant y pwll, plant y pwll.*"

I gave Roberts no time for reflection. I woke him up, bustled him out of bed, hurried him through his breakfast, saw him pack his suitcase, make his farewells to the Morgans, and had him sitting in the shade on Nichol's lawn well before the family were back from church. I gave Nichol a vague outline of the circumstances—nervous breakdown and so forth—introduced them to one another, and left them talking about the Black Mountains, Roberts's land of origin. The next day I saw him off at the station, on his way to Great Yarmouth, via London. I told him with an air of authority that he would have no more trouble, "from any quarter," I emphasized. And he was to write to me at my town address in a week's time.

"And, by the way," I said, Just before the train slid along the platform, "here's a bit of Welsh for you. What does *'plant y pwll'* mean? Something of the pool?"

"'*Plant y pwll,*'" he explained, "means 'children of the pool.'"

When my holiday was ended, and I had got back to town. I began my investigations into the case of James Roberts and his nocturnal visitant. When he began his story I was extremely distressed—I made no doubt as to the bare truth of it, and was shocked to think of a very kindly man threatened with overwhelming disgrace and disaster. There seemed nothing impossible in the tale stated at large, and in the first outline. It is not altogether unheard of for very decent men to have had a black patch in their lives, which they have done their best to live down and atone for and forget. Often enough, the explanation of such misadventure is not hard to seek. You have a young fellow, very decently but very simply brought up among simple country people, suddenly pitched into the labyrinth of London, into a maze in which there are many turnings, as the unfortunate Roberts put it, which lead to disaster, or to something blacker than disaster. The more experienced man, the man of keen instincts and perceptions, knows the aspect of these tempting passages and avoids them; some have the wit to turn back in time; a few are caught in the trap at the end. And in some cases, though there may be apparent escape, and peace and security for many years, the teeth of the snare are about the man's leg all the while, and close at last on highly reputable chairmen and churchwardens and pillars of all sorts of seemly institutions. And then goal, or at best, hissing and extinction.

So, on the first face of it, I was by no means prepared to pooh-pooh Robert's tale. But when he came to detail, and I had time to think it over, that entirely illogical faculty, which sometimes takes charge of our thoughts and judgments, told me that there was some huge flaw in all this, that somehow or other, things had not happened so. This mental process, I may say, is strictly indefinable and unjustifiable by any laws of thought that I have ever heard of. It won't do to take our stand with Bishop Butler, and declare with him that probability is the guide of life; deducing from this premise the conclusion that the improbable doesn't happen. Any man who cares to glance over his experience of the world and of things in general is aware that the most wildly improbable events are constantly happening. For example, I take up to-day's paper, sure that I shall find something to my purpose, and in a minute I come across the headline: "Damaging a Model Elephant." A father, evidently a man of substance, accuses his son of this strange offence. Last summer, the father told the court, his son constructed in their front garden a large model of an elephant, the material being bought by witness. The skeleton of the elephant was made of tubing, and it was covered with soil and fiber, and held together with wire netting. Flowers were planted on it, and it cost £3 5s.

A photograph of the elephant was produced in court, and the clerk remarked: "It is a fearsome-looking thing."

And then the catastrophe. The son got to know a married woman much older than himself, and his parents frowned, and there were quarrels. And so, one night, the young man came to his father's house, jumped over the garden wall and tried to push the elephant over. Failing, he proceeded to disembowel the elephant with a pair of wire clippers.

There! Nothing can be much more improbable than that tale, but it all happened so, as the *Daily Telegraph* assures me, and I believe every word of it. And I have no doubt that if I care to look I shall find something as improbable, or even more improbable, in the newspaper columns three or perhaps four times a week. What about the old man, unknown, unidentified, found in the Thames: in one pocket, a stone Buddha; in the other, a leather wallet, with the inscription: "The hen that sits on the china egg is best off?"

The improbable happens and is constantly happening; but, using that faculty which I am unable to define, I rejected Roberts's girl of the wood and the window. I did not suspect him for a moment of leg-pulling of an offensive and vicious kind. His misery and terror were too clearly manifest for that, and I was certain that he was suffering from a very serious and dreadful shock—and yet I didn't believe in the truth of the story he had told me. I felt convinced that there was no girl in the case; either in the wood or at the window. And when Roberts told me, with increased horror, that every word she spoke was true, that she had even reminded him of matters that he had himself forgotten, I was greatly encouraged in my growing surmise. For, it seemed to me at least probable that if the case had been such as he supposed it, there would have been new and damning circumstances in the story, utterly unknown to him and unsuspected by him. But, as it was, everything that he was told he accepted; as a man in a dream accepts without hesitation the wildest fantasies as matters and incidents of his daily experience. Decidedly, there was no girl there.

On the Sunday that he spent with me at the Wern, Nichol's place, I took advantage of his calmer condition—the night's rest had done him good—to get some facts and dates out of him, and when I returned to town, I put these to the test. It was not altogether an easy investigation since, on the surface, at least, the matters to be investigated were eminently trivial; the early days of a young man from the country up in London in a business house; and twenty-five years ago. Even really exciting murder trials and changes of ministries become blurred and uncertain in outline, if not forgotten, in twenty-five years, or in twelve years for that matter: and compared with such events, the affair of James Roberts seemed perilously like nothing at all.

However, I had made the best use I could of the information that Roberts had given me; and I was fortified for the task by a letter I received from him. He told me that there had been no recurrence of the trouble (as he expressed it), that he felt quite well, and was enjoying himself immensely at Yarmouth. He said that the shows and entertainments on the sands were doing him "no end of good. There's a retired executioner who does his old business in a tent, with the drop and everything. And there's a bloke who calls himself Archbishop of London, who fasts in a glass case, with his mitre and all his togs on." Certainly, my patient was either recovered, or in a very fair way to recovery: I could set about my researches in a calm spirit of scientific curiosity, without the nervous tension of the surgeon called upon at short notice to perform a life-or-death operation.

As a matter of fact it was all simpler than I thought it would be. True, the results were nothing, or almost nothing, but that was exactly what I had expected and hoped. With the slight sketch of his early career in London, furnished me by Roberts, the horrors omitted by my request; with a name or two and a date or two, I got along very well. And what did it come to? Simply this: here was a lad—he was just seventeen—who had been brought up amongst lonely hills and educated at a small grammar school, furnished through a London uncle with a very small stool in a City office. By arrangement, settled after a long and elaborate correspondence, he was to board with some distant cousins, who lived in the Cricklewood-Kilburn-Brondesbury region, and with them he settled down, comfortably enough, as it seemed, though Cousin Ellen objected to his learning to smoke in his bedroom, and begged him to desist. The household consisted of Cousin Ellen, her husband, Henry Watts, and the two daughters, Helen and Justine. Justine was about Robert's own age; Helen three or four years older. Mr. Watts had married rather late in life, and had retired from his office a year or so before. He interested himself chiefly in tuberous-rooted begonias, and in the season went out a few miles to his cricket club and watched the game on Saturday afternoons. Every morning there was breakfast at eight, every evening there was high tea at seven, and in the meantime young Roberts did his best in the City, and liked his job well enough. He was shy with the two girls at first, but Justine was lively, and couldn't help having a voice like a peacock, and Helen was adorable. And so things went on very pleasantly for a year or perhaps eighteen months; on this basis, that Justine was a great joke, and that Helen was adorable. The trouble was that Justine didn't think she was a great joke.

For, it must be said that Roberts's stay with his cousins ended in disaster. I rather gather that the young man and the quiet Helen were guilty of—shall, we say—amiable indiscretions, though without serious consequences. But it appeared that Cousin Justine, a girl with black eyes and black hair, made discoveries which she resented savagely, denouncing the offenders at the top of that piercing voice of hers, in the waste hours of the Brondesbury night, to the immense rage, horror, and consternation of the whole house. In fact, there was the devil to pay, and Mr. Watts then and there turned young Roberts out of the house. And there is no doubt that he should have been thoroughly ashamed of himself. But young men....

Nothing very much happened. Old Watts had cried in his rage that he would let Roberts's chief in the City hear the whole story; but, on reflection, he held his tongue. Roberts roamed about London for the rest of the night, refreshing himself occasionally at coffee-stalls. When the shops opened, he had a wash and brush-up, and was prompt and bright at his office. At midday, in the underground smoking-room of the tea-shop, he conferred with a fellow clerk over their dominoes, and arranged to share rooms with him out Norwood way. From that point onwards, the career of James Roberts had been eminently quiet, uneventful, successful.

Now, everybody, I suppose, is aware that in recent years the silly business of divination by dreams has ceased to be a joke and has become a very serious science. It is called "Psycho-analysis"; and is compounded, I would say, by mingling one grain of sense with a hundred of pure nonsense. From the simplest and most obvious dreams, the psycho-analyst deduces the most incongruous and extravagant results. A black savage tells him that he has dreamed of being chased by lions, or, maybe, by crocodiles: and the psycho man knows at once that the black is suffering from the *Œdipus* complex. That is, he is madly in love with his own mother, and is, therefore, afraid of the vengeance of his father. Everybody knows, of course, that "lion" and "crocodile" are symbols of "father." And I understand that there are educated people who believe this stuff.

It is all nonsense, to be sure; and so much the greater nonsense inasmuch as the true interpretation of many dreams—not by any means of all dreams—moves, it may be said, in the opposite direction to the method of psycho-analysis. The psycho-analyst infers the monstrous and abnormal from a trifle; it is often safe to reverse the process. If a man dreams that he has committed a sin before which the sun hid his face, it is often safe to conjecture that, in sheer forgetfulness, he wore a red tie, or brown boots with evening dress. A slight dispute with the vicar may deliver him in sleep into the clutches of the Spanish Inquisition, and the torment of a fiery death. Failure to catch the post with a rather important letter will sometimes bring a great realm to ruin in the world of dreams. And here, I have no doubt, we have the explanation of part of the explanation of the Roberts affair. Without question, he had been a bad boy; there was something more than a trifle at the heart of his trouble. But his original offence, grave as we may think it, had in his hidden consciousness, swollen and exaggerated itself into a monstrous mythology of evil. Some time ago, a learned and curious investigator demonstrated how Coleridge had taken a bald sentence from an old chronicler, and had made it the nucleus of *The Ancient Mariner*. With a vast gesture of the spirit, he had uncon-

sciously gathered from all the four seas of his vast reading all manner of creatures into his net: till the bare hint of the old book
glowed into one of the great masterpieces of the world's poetry.
Roberts had nothing in him of the poetic faculty, nothing of the
shaping power of the imagination, no trace of the gift of expression, by which the artist delivers his soul of its burden. In him, as
in many men, there was a great gulf fixed between the hidden and
the open consciousness; so that which could not come out into the
light grew and swelled secretly, hugely, horribly in the darkness. If
Roberts had been a poet or a painter or a musician; we might have
had a masterpiece. As he was neither: we had a monster. And I do
not at all believe that his years had consciously been vexed by a
deep sense of guilt. I gathered in the course of my researches that
not long after the flight from Brondesbury, Roberts was made
aware of unfortunate incidents in the Watts saga—if we may use
this honoured term—which convinced him that there were extenu-
ating circumstances in his offence, and excuses for his wrongdoing.
The actual fact had, no doubt, been forgotten or remembered very
slightly, rarely, casually, without any sense of grave moment or cul-
pability attached to it; while, all the while, a pageantry of horror
was being secretly formed in the hidden places of the man's soul.
And at last, after the years of growth and swelling in the darkness;
the monster leapt into the light, and with such violence that to the
victim it seemed an actual and objective entity.

And, in a sense, it had risen from the black waters of the
pool. I was reading a few days ago, in a review of a grave book on
psychology, the following very striking sentences:

The things which we distinguish as qualities or values are
inherent in the real environment to make the configuration that
they do make with our sensory response to them. There is such a
thing as a "sad" landscape, even when we who look at it are feeling
jovial; and if we think it is "sad" only because we attribute to it
something derived from our own past associations with sadness,

Professor Koffka gives us good reason to regard the view as superficial. That is not imputing human attributes to what are described as "demand characters" in the environment, but giving proper recognition to the other end of a nexus, of which only one end is organised in our own mind.

Psychology is, I am sure, a difficult and subtle science, which, perhaps naturally, must be expressed in subtle and difficult language. But so far as I can gather the sense of the passage which I have quoted, it comes to, this: that a landscape, a certain configuration of wood, water, height and depth, light and dark, flower and rock, is, in fact, an objective reality, a thing; just as opium and wine are things, not clotted fancies, mere creatures of our make-believe, to which we give a kind of spurious reality and efficacy. The dreams of De Quincey were a synthesis of De Quincey, *plus* opium; the riotous gaiety of Charles Surface and his friends was the product and result of the wine they had drunk, plus their personalities. So, the profound Professor Koffka—his book is called *Principles of Gestalt Psychology*—insists that the "sadness" which we attribute to a particular landscape is really and efficiently in the landscape and not merely in ourselves; and consequently that the landscape can affect us and produce results in us, in precisely the same manner as drugs and meat and drink affect us in their several ways. Poe, who knew many secrets, knew this, and taught that landscape gardening was as truly a fine art as poetry or painting; since it availed to communicate the mysteries to the human spirit.

And perhaps, Mrs. Morgan of Lanypwll Farm put all this much better in the speech of symbolism, when she murmured about the children of the pool. For if there is a landscape of sadness, there is certainly also a landscape of a horror of darkness and evil; and that black and oily depth, overshadowed with twisted woods, with its growth of foul weeds and, its dead trees and leprous boughs was assuredly potent in terror. To Roberts it was a strong drug, a drag of evocation; the black deep without calling to the black deep within, and summoning the inhabitant thereof to come forth. I made no attempt to extract the legend of that dark place from Mrs. Morgan; and I do not suppose that she would have been communicative if I had questioned her. But it has struck me as possible and even probable that Roberts was by no means the first to experience the power of the pool. Old stories often turn out to be true.

THE END

*

# THE INMOST
# LIGHT

# I

One evening in autumn, when the deformities of London were veiled in faint blue mist, and its vistas and far-reaching streets seemed splendid, Mr. Charles Salisbury was slowly pacing down Rupert Street, drawing nearer to his favourite restaurant by slow degrees. His eyes were downcast in study of the pavement, and thus it was that as he passed in at the narrow door a man who had come up from the lower end of the street jostled against him.

"I beg your pardon—wasn't looking where I was going. Why, it's Dyson!"

"Yes, quite so. How are you, Salisbury?"

"Quite well. But where have you been, Dyson? I don't think I can have seen you for the last five years?"

"No; I dare say not. You remember I was getting rather hard up when you came to my place at Charlotte Street?"

"Perfectly. I think I remember your telling me that you owed five weeks' rent, and that you had parted with your watch for a comparatively small sum."

"My dear Salisbury, your memory is admirable. Yes, I was hard up. But the curious thing is that soon after you saw me I became harder up. My financial state was described by a friend as 'stone broke.' I don't approve of slang, mind you, but such was my condition. But suppose we go in; there might be other people who would like to dine—it's human weakness, Salisbury."

"Certainly; come along. I was wondering as I walked down whether the corner table was taken. It has a velvet back you know."

"I know the spot; it's vacant. Yes, as I was saying, I became even harder up."

"What did you do then?" asked Salisbury, disposing of his hat, and settling down in the corner of the seat, with a glance of fond anticipation at the menu.

"What did I do? Why, I sat down and reflected. I had a good classical education, and a positive distaste for business of any kind: that was the capital with which I faced the world. Do you know, I have heard people describe olives as nasty! What lamentable Philistinism! I have often thought, Salisbury, that I could write genuine poetry under the influence of olives and red wine.

Let us have Chianti; it may not be very good, but the flasks are simply charming."

"It is pretty good here. We may as well have a big flask."

"Very good. I reflected, then, on my want of prospects, and I determined to embark in literature."

"Really; that was strange. You seem in pretty comfortable circumstances, though."

"Though! What a satire upon a noble profession. I am afraid, Salisbury, you haven't a proper idea of the dignity of an artist. You see me sitting at my desk—or at least you can see me if you care to call—with pen and ink, and simple nothingness before me, and if you come again in a few hours you will (in all probability) find a creation!"

"Yes, quite so. I had an idea that literature was not remunerative."

"You are mistaken; its rewards are great. I may mention, by the way, that shortly after you saw me I succeeded to a small income. An uncle died, and proved unexpectedly generous."

"Ah, I see. That must have been convenient."."It was pleasant—undeniably pleasant. I have always considered it in the light of an endowment of my researches. I told you I was a man of letters; it would, perhaps, be more correct to describe myself as a man of science."

"Dear me, Dyson, you have really changed very much in the last few years. I had a notion, don't you know, that you were a sort of idler about town, the kind of man one might meet on the north side of Piccadilly every day from May to July."

"Exactly. I was even then forming myself, though all un-consciously. You know my poor father could not afford to send me to the University. I used to grumble in my ignorance at not having completed my education. That was the folly of youth, Salis-bury; my University was Piccadilly.

There I began to study the great science which still occu-pies me."

"What science do you mean?"

"The science of the great city; the physiology of London; literally and metaphysically the greatest subject that the mind of man can conceive. What an admirable salmi this us; undoubtedly the final end of the pheasant. Yet I feel sometimes positively over-whelmed with the thought of the vastness and complexity of London. Paris a man may get to understand thoroughly with a rea-sonable amount of study; but London is always a mystery. In Paris you may say: 'Here live the actresses, here the Bohemians, and the Ratés'; but it is different in London. You may point out a street, correctly enough, as the abode of washerwomen; but, in that sec-ond floor, a man may be studying Chaldee roots, and in the garret over the way a forgotten artist is dying by inches."

"I see you are Dyson, unchanged and unchangeable," said Salisbury, slowly sipping his Chianti. "I think you are misled by a too fervid imagination; the mystery of London exists only in your fancy. It seems to me a dull place enough. We seldom hear of a really artistic crime in London, whereas I believe Paris abounds in that sort of thing."

"Give me some more wine. Thanks. You are mistaken, my dear fellow, you are really mistaken. London has nothing to be ashamed of in the way of crime. Where we fail is for want of

Homers, not Agamemnons. Carent quia vate sacro, you know."

"I recall the quotation. But I don't think I quite follow you."

"Well, in plain language, we have no good writers in London who make a speciality of that kind of thing. Our common reporter is a dull dog; every story that he has to tell is spoilt in the telling. His idea of horror and of what excites horror is so lamentably deficient. Nothing will content the fellow but blood, vulgar red blood, and when he can get it he lays it on thick, and considers that he has produced a telling article. It's a poor notion. And, by some curious fatality, it is the most commonplace and brutal murders which always attract the most attention and get written up the most. For instance, I dare say that you never heard of the Harlesden case?"

"No; no, I don't remember anything about it."

"Of course not. And yet the story is a curious one. I will tell you over our coffee. Harlesden, you know, or I expect you don't know, is quite on the out-quarters of London; something curiously different from your fine old crusted suburb like Norwood or Hampstead, different as each of these is from the other. Hampstead, I mean, is where you look for the head of your great China house with his three acres of land and pine-houses, though of late there is the artistic substratum; while Norwood is the home of the prosperous middle-class family who took the house 'because it was near the Palace,' and sickened of the Palace six months afterwards; but Harlesden is a place of no character. It's too new to have any character as yet. There are the rows of red houses and the rows of white houses and the bright green Venetians, and the blistering doorways, and the little backyards they call gardens, and a few feeble shops, and then, just as you think you're going to grasp the physiognomy of the settlement, it all melts away."

"How the dickens is that? The houses don't tumble down before one's eyes, I suppose!"

"Well, no, not exactly that. But Harlesden as an entity disappears. Your street turns into a quiet lane, and your staring houses into elm trees, and the back-gardens into green meadows. You pass instantly from town to country; there is no transition as in a small country town, no soft gradations of wider lawns and orchards, with houses gradually becoming less dense, but a dead stop. I believe the people who live there mostly go into the City. I have seen once or twice a laden bus bound thitherwards. But however that may be, I can't conceive a greater loneliness in a desert at midnight than there is there at midday. It is like a city of the dead; the streets are glaring and desolate, and as you pass it suddenly strikes you that this too is part of London. Well, a year or two ago there was a doctor living there; he had set up his brass plate and his red lamp at the very end of one of those shining streets, and from the back of the house, the fields stretched away to the north. I don't know what his reason was in settling down in such an out-of-the-way place, perhaps Dr. Black, as we call him, was a far-seeing man and looked ahead. His relations, so it appeared afterwards, had lost sight of him for many years and didn't even know he was a doctor, much less where he lived. However, there he was settled in Harlesden, with some fragments of a practice, and an uncommonly pretty wife. People used to see them walking out together in the summer evenings soon after they came to Harlesden, and, so far as could be observed, they seemed a very affectionate couple. These walks went on through the autumn, and then ceased, but, of course, as the days grew dark and the weather cold, the lanes near Harlesden might be expected to lose many of their attractions. All through the winter nobody saw anything of Mrs.

Black, the doctor used to reply to his patients' inquiries that she was a 'little out of sorts, would be better, no doubt, in the spring.' But the spring came, and the summer, and no Mrs. Black appeared, and at last people began to rumour and talk amongst themselves, and all sorts of queer things were said at 'high teas,' which you may possibly have heard are the only form of entertainment known in such suburbs. Dr. Black began to surprise some very odd looks cast in his direction, and the practice, such as it was, fell off before his eyes. In short, when the neighbours whispered about the matter, they whispered that Mrs. Black was dead, and that the doctor had made away with her. But this wasn't the case; Mrs. Black was seen alive in June. It was a Sunday afternoon, one of those few exquisite days that an English climate offers, and half London had strayed out into the fields, north, south, east, and west to smell the scent of the white May, and to see if the wild roses were yet in blossom in the hedges. I had gone out myself early in the morning, and had had a long ramble, and somehow or other as I was steering homeward I found myself in this very Harlesden we have been talking about. To be exact, I had a glass of beer in the General Gordon, the most flourishing house in the neighbourhood, and as I was wandering rather aimlessly about, I saw an uncommonly tempting gap in a hedgerow, and resolved to explore the meadow beyond. Soft grass is very grateful to the feet after the infernal grit strewn on suburban sidewalks, and after walking about for some time I thought I should like to sit down on a bank and have a smoke. While I was getting out my pouch, I looked up in the direction of the houses, and as I looked I felt my breath caught back, and my teeth began to chatter, and the stick I had in one hand snapped in two with the grip I gave it. It was as if I had had an electric current down my spine, and yet for some moment of time which seemed long, but which must have been very short, I caught myself wondering what on earth was the matter. Then I knew I what had made my very heart shudder and my bones grind together in an agony. As I glanced up I had looked straight towards the last house in the row before me, and in an upper window of that house I had seen for some short fraction of a second a face. It was the face of a woman, and yet it was not human. You and I, Salisbury, have heard in our time, as we sat in our seats in church in sober English fashion, of a lust that cannot be satiated and of a fire that is unquenchable, but few of us have any notion what these words mean. I hope you never may, for as I saw that face at the window, with the blue sky above me and the warm air playing in gusts about me, I knew I had looked into another world—looked through the window of a commonplace, brand-new house, and seen hell open before me. When the first shock was over, I thought once or twice that I should have fainted; my face streamed with a cold sweat, and my breath came and went in sobs, as if I had been half drowned. I managed to get up at last, and walk round to the street, and there I saw the name 'Dr. Black' on the post by the front gate. As fate or my luck would have it, the door opened and a man came down the steps as I passed by. I had no doubt it was the doctor himself. He was of a type rather common in London; long and thin, with a pasty face and a dull black moustache. He gave me a look as we passed each other on the pavement, and though it was merely the casual glance which one foot-passenger bestows on another, I felt convinced in my mind that here was an ugly customer to deal with. As you may imagine, I went my way a good deal puzzled and horrified too by what I had seen; for I had paid another visit to the General Gordon, and had got together a good deal of the common gossip of the place about the Blacks. I didn't mention the fact that I had seen a woman's face in the window; but I heard that Mrs. Black had been much admired for her beautiful golden hair, and round what had struck me with such a nameless terror, there was a mist of flowing yellow hair, as it was an aureole of glory round the visage of a satyr. The whole thing bothered me in an indescribable manner; and when I got home I tried my best to think of the impression I had received as an illusion, but it was no use. I knew very well I had seen what I have tried to describe to you, and I was morally certain that I had seen Mrs. Black. And then there was the gossip of the place, the suspicion of foul play, which I knew to be false, and my own conviction that there was some deadly mischief or other going on in that bright red house at the corner of Devon Road: how to construct a theory of a reasonable kind out of these two elements. In short, I found myself in a world of mystery; I puzzled my head over it and filled up my leisure moments by gathering together odd threads of speculation, but I never moved a step towards any real solution, and as the summer days went on the matter seemed to grow misty and indistinct, shadowing some vague terror, like a nightmare of last month. I suppose it would before long have faded into the background of my brain—I should not have forgotten it, for such a thing could never be forgotten—but one morning as I was looking over the paper my eye was caught by a heading over some two dozen lines of small type. The words I had seen were simply: 'The Harlesden Case,' and I knew what I was going to read. Mrs. Black was dead. Black had called in another medical man to certify as to cause of death, and something or other had aroused the strange doctor's suspicions and there had been an inquest and post-mortem. And the result? That, I will confess, did astonish me considerably; it was the triumph of the unexpected. The two doctors who made the autopsy were obliged to confess that they could not discover the faintest trace of any kind of foul play; their most exquisite tests and reagents failed to detect the presence of poison in the most infinitesimal quantity. Death, they found, had been caused by a somewhat obscure and scientifically interesting form of brain disease. The tissue of the brain and the molecules of the grey matter had undergone a most extraordinary series of changes; and the younger of the two doctors, who has some reputation, I believe, as a specialist in brain trouble, made some remarks in giving his evidence which struck me deeply at the time, though I did not then grasp their full significance. He said: 'At the commencement of the examination I was astonished to find appearances of a character entirely new to me, notwithstanding my somewhat large experience. I need not specify these appearances at present, it will be sufficient for me to state that as I proceeded in my task I could scarcely believe that the brain before me was that of a human being at all.' There was some surprise at this statement, as you may imagine, and the coroner asked the doctor if he meant that the brain resembled that of an animal. 'No,' he replied, 'I should not put it in that way. Some of the appearances I noticed seemed to point in that direction, but others, and these were the more surprising, indicated a nervous organization of a wholly different character from that either of man or the lower animals.' It was a curious thing to say, but of course the jury brought in a verdict of death from natural causes, and, so far as the public was concerned, the case came to an end. But after I had read what the doctor said I made up my mind that I should like to know a good deal more, and I set to work on what seemed likely to prove an interesting investigation. I had really a good deal of trouble, but I was successful in a measure. Though why—my dear fellow, I had no notion at the time. Are you aware that we have been here nearly four hours? The waiters are staring at us. Let's have the bill and be gone."

The two men went out in silence, and stood a moment in the cool air, watching the hurrying traffic of Coventry Street pass before them to the accompaniment of the ringing bells of hansoms and the cries of the newsboys; the deep far murmur of London surging up ever and again from beneath these louder noises.

"It is a strange case, isn't it?" said Dyson at length. "What do you think of it?"

"My dear fellow. I haven't heard the end, so I will reserve my opinion. When will you give me the sequel?"

"Come to my rooms some evening; say next Thursday. Here's the address. Good-night; I want to get down to the Strand." Dyson hailed a passing hansom, and Salisbury turned northward to walk home to his lodgings.

# II

Mr. Salisbury, as may have been gathered from the few remarks which he had found it possible to introduce in the course of
the evening, was a young gentleman of a peculiarly solid form of
intellect, coy and retiring before the mysterious and the uncommon, with a constitutional dislike of paradox. During the
restaurant dinner he had been forced to listen in almost absolute
silence to a strange tissue of improbabilities strung together with
the ingenuity of a born meddler in plots and mysteries, and it was
with a feeling of weariness that he crossed Shaftesbury Avenue,
and dived into the recesses of Soho, for his lodgings were in a
modest neighbourhood to the north of Oxford Street. As he
walked he speculated on the probable fate of Dyson, relying on
literature, unbefriended by a thoughtful relative, and could not help
concluding that so much subtlety united to a too vivid imagination
would in all likelihood have been rewarded with a pair of sand-
wich-boards or a super's banner. Absorbed in this train of thought,
and admiring the perverse dexterity which could transmute the face
of a sickly woman and a case of brain disease into the crude elements of romance, Salisbury strayed on through the dimly lighted
streets, not noticing the gusty wind which drove sharply round
corners and whirled the stray rubbish of the pavement into the air
in eddies, while black clouds gathered over the sickly yellow moon.
Even a stray drop or two of rain blown into his face did not rouse
him from his meditations, and it was only when with a sudden rush
the storm tore down upon the street that he began to consider the
expediency of finding some shelter. The rain, driven by the wind,
pelted down with the violence of a thunderstorm, dashing up from
the stones and hissing through the air, and soon a perfect torrent
of water coursed along the kennels and accumulated in pools over
the choked-up drains.

The few stray passengers who had been loafing rather than

walking about the street had scuttered away, like frightened rabbits, to some invisible places of refuge, and though Salisbury whistled loud and long for a hansom, no hansom appeared. He looked about him, as if to discover how far he might be from the haven of Oxford Street, but strolling carelessly along, he had turned out of his way, and found himself in an unknown region, and one to all appearance devoid even of a public house where shelter could be bought for the modest sum of two pence. The street lamps were few and at-long intervals, and burned behind grimy glasses with the sickly light of oil, and by this wavering glimmer Salisbury could make out the shadowy and vast old~ houses of which the street was composed. As he passed along, hurrying, and shrinking from the full sweep of the rain, he noticed the innumerable bell-handles, with names that seemed about to vanish of old age graven on brass plates beneath them, and here and there a richly carved penthouse overhung the door, blackening with the grime of fifty years. The storm seemed to grow more and more furious; he was wet through, and a new hat had become a ruin, and still Oxford Street seemed as far off as ever; it was with deep relief that the dripping man caught sight of a dark archway which seemed to promise shelter from the rain if not from the wind. Salisbury took up his position in the driest corner and looked about him; he was standing in a kind of passage contrived under part of a house, and behind him stretched a narrow footway leading between blank walls to regions unknown. He had stood there for some time, vainly endeavouring to rid himself of some of his superfluous moisture, and listening for the passing wheel of a hansom, when his attention was aroused by a loud noise coming from the direction of the passage behind, and growing louder as it drew nearer. In a couple of minutes he could make out the shrill, raucous voice of a woman, threatening and renouncing and making the very stones echo with her accents, while now and then a man grumbled and expostulated. Though to all appearance devoid of romance, Salisbury had some relish for street rows, and was, indeed, somewhat of an amateur in the more amusing phases of drunkenness; he therefore composed himself to listen and observe with something of the air of a subscriber to grand opera. To his annoyance, however, the tempest seemed suddenly to be composed, and he could hear nothing but the impatient steps of the woman and the slow lurch of the man as they came towards him. Keeping back in the shadow of the wall, he could see the two drawing nearer; the man was evidently drunk, and had much ado to avoid frequent collision with the wall as he tacked across from one side to the other, like some bark beating up against a wind. The woman was looking straight in front of her, with tears streaming from her blazing eyes, but suddenly as they went by the flame blazed up again, and she burst forth into a torrent of abuse, facing round upon her companion.

"You low rascal, you mean, comtemptible cur," she went on, after an incoherent storm of curses, "you think I'm to work and slave for you always, I suppose, while you're after that Green Street girl and drinking every penny you've got? But you're mistaken, Sam—indeed, I'll bear it no longer. Damn you, you dirty thief, I've done with you and your master too, so you can go your own errands, and I only hope they'll get you into trouble."

The woman tore at the bosom of her dress, and taking something out that looked like paper, crumpled it up and flung it away. It fell at Salisbury's feet. She ran out and disappeared in the darkness, while the man lurched slowly into the street, grumbling indistinctly to himself in a perplexed tone of voice. Salisbury looked out after him, and saw him maundering along the pavement, halting now and then and swaying indecisively, and then starting off at some fresh tangent. The sky had cleared, and white fleecy clouds were fleeting across the moon, high in the heaven. The light came and went by turns, as the clouds passed by, and, turning round as the.clear, white rays shone into the passage, Salisbury saw the little ball of crumpled paper which the woman had cast down. Oddly curious to know what it might contain, he picked it up and put it in his pocket, and set out afresh on his journey.

# III

Salisbury was a man of habit. When he got home, drenched to the skin, his clothes hanging lank about him, and a ghastly dew besmearing his hat, his only thought was of his health, of which he took studious care. So, after changing his clothes and encasing himself in a warm dressing-gown, he proceeded to prepare a sudorific in the shape of hot gin and water, warming the latter over one of those spirit-lamps which mitigate the austerities of the modern hermit's life. By the time this preparation had been exhibited, and Salisbury's disturbed feelings had been soothed by a pipe of tobacco, he was able to get into bed in a happy state of vacancy, without a thought of his adventure in the dark archway, or of the weird fancies with which Dyson had seasoned his dinner. It was the same at breakfast the next morning, for Salisbury made a point of not thinking of anything until that meal was over; but when the cup and saucer were cleared away, and the morning pipe was lit, he remembered the little ball of paper, and began fumbling in the pockets of his wet coat. He did not remember into which pocket he had put it, and as he dived now into one and now into another, he experienced a strange feeling of apprehension lest it should not be there at all, though he could not for the life of him have explained the importance he attached to what was in all probability mere rubbish. But he sighed with relief when his fingers touched the crumpled surface in an inside pocket, and he drew it out gently and laid it on the little desk by his easy chair with as much care as if it had been some rare jewel. Salisbury sat smoking and staring at his find for a few minutes, an odd temptation to throw the thing in the fire and have done with it struggling with as odd a speculation as to its possible contents, and as to the reason why the infuriated woman should have flung a bit of paper from her with such vehemence. As might be expected, it was the latter feeling that conquered in the end, and yet it was with something like repugnance that he at last took the paper and unrolled it, and laid it out before him. It was a piece of common dirty paper, to all appearance torn out of a cheap exercise book, and in the middle were a few lines written in a queer cramped hand. Salisbury bent his head and stared eagerly at it for a moment, drawing a long breath, and then fell back in his chair gazing blankly before him, till at last with a sudden revulsion he burst into a peal of laughter, so long and loud and uproarious that the landlady's baby in the floor below awoke from sleep and echoed his mirth with hideous yells. But he laughed again and again, and took the paper up to read a second time what seemed such meaningless nonsense.

"Q. has had to go and see his friends in Paris," it began. "Traverse Handel S. 'Once around the grass, and twice around the lass, and thrice around the maple-tree.' "

Salisbury took up the paper and crumpled it as the angry woman had done, and aimed it at the fire. He did not throw it there, however, but tossed it carelessly into the well of the desk, and laughed again. The sheer folly of the thing offended him, and he was ashamed of his own eager speculation, as one who pores over the high-sounding announcements in the agony column of the daily paper, and finds nothing but advertisement and triviality. He walked to the window, and stared out at the languid morning life of his quarter; the maids in slatternly print dresses washing door-steps, the fish-monger and the butcher on their rounds, and the tradesmen standing at the doors of their small shops, drooping for lack of trade and excitement. In the distance a blue haze gave some grandeur to the prospect, but the view as a whole was depressing, and would only have interested a student of the life of London, who finds something rare and choice in its every aspect. Salisbury turned away in disgust, and settled himself in the easy chair, upholstered in a bright shade of green, and decked with yellow gimp, which was the pride and attraction of the apartments. Here he composed himself to his morning's occupation—the perusal of a novel that dealt with sport and love in a manner that suggested the collaboration of a stud-groom and a ladies' college. In an ordinary way, however, Salisbury would have been carried on by the interest of the story up to lunch time, but this morning he fidgeted in and out of his chair, took the book up and laid it down again, and swore at last to himself and at himself in mere irritation.

In point of fact the jingle of the paper found in the arch-way had "got into his head," and do what he would he could not help muttering over and over, "Once around the grass, and twice around the lass, and thrice around the maple-tree." It became a positive pain, like the foolish burden of a music-hall song, everlast-ingly quoted, and sung at all hours of the day and night, and treasured by the street boys as an unfailing resource for six months together. He went out into the streets, and tried to forget his en-emy in the jostling of the crowds and the roar and clatter of the traffic, but presently he would find himself stealing quietly aside, and pacing some deserted byway.

Vainly puzzling his brains, and trying to fix some meaning to phrases that were meaningless. It was a positive relief when Thursday came, and he remembered that he had made an ap-pointment to go and see Dyson; the flimsy reveries of the self-styled man of letters appeared entertaining when compared with this ceaseless iteration, this maze of thought from which there seemed no possibility of escape. Dyson's abode was in one of the quietest of the quiet streets that lead down from the Strand to the river, and when Salisbury passed from the narrow stairway into his friend's room, he saw that the uncle had been beneficent indeed. The floor glowed and flamed with all the colours of the East; it was, as Dyson pompously remarked, "a sunset in a dream," and the lamplight, the twilight of London streets, was shut out with strangely worked curtains, glittering here and there with threads of gold. In the shelves of an oak armoire stood jars and plates of old French china, and the black and white of etchings not to be found in the Haymarket or in Bond Street, stood out against the splendour of a Japanese paper. Salisbury sat down on the settle by the hearth, and sniffed and mingled fumes of incense and tobacco, wondering and dumb before all this splendour after the green rep and the oleographs, the gilt-framed mirror, and the lustres of his own apartment.

"I am glad you have come, ' said Dyson. "Comfortable little room, isn't it? But you don't look very well, Salisbury. Nothing disagreed with you, has it?"

"No; but I have been a good deal bothered for the last few days. The fact is I had an odd kind of—of—adventure, I suppose I may call it, that night I saw you, and it has worried me a good deal. And the provoking part of it is that it's the merest nonsense—but, however, I will tell you all about it, by and by. You were going to let me have the rest of that odd story you began at the restaurant."

"Yes. But I am afraid, Salisbury, you are incorrigible. You are a slave to what you call matter of fact. You know perfectly well that in your heart you think the oddness in that case is of my making, and that it is all really as plain as the police reports. However, as I have begun, I will go on. But first we will have something to drink, and you may as well light your pipe."

Dyson went up to the oak cupboard, and drew from its depths a rotund bottle and two little glasses, quaintly gilded.

"It's Benedictine," he said. "You'll have some, won't you?"

Salisbury assented, and the two men sat sipping and smoking reflectively for some minutes before Dyson began.."Let me see," he said at lasts "we were at the inquest, weren't we? No, we had done with that.

Ah, I remember. I was telling you that on the whole I had been successful in my inquiries, investigation, or whatever you like to call it, into the matter. Wasn't that where I left off?"

"Yes, that was it. To be precise, I think 'though' was the last word you said on the matter."

"Exactly. I have been thinking it all over since the other night, and I have come to the conclusion that that 'though' is a very big 'though' indeed. Not to put too fine a point on it, I have had to confess that what I found out, or thought I found out, amounts in reality to nothing. I am as far away from the heart of the case as ever. However, I may as well tell you what I do know. You may remember my saying that I was impressed a good deal by some remarks of one of the doctors who gave evidence at the inquest. Well, I determined that my first step must be to try if I could get something more definite and intelligible out of that doctor. Somehow or other I managed to get an introduction to the man, and he gave me an appointment to come and see him.

He turned out to be a pleasant, genial fellow; rather young and not in the least like the typical medical man, and he began the conference by offering me whisky and cigars. I didn't think it worthwhile to beat about the bush, so I began by saying that part of his evidence at the Harlesden inquest struck me as very peculiar, and I gave him the printed report, with the sentences in question underlined. He just glanced at the slip, and gave me a queer look. 'It struck you as peculiar, did it?" said he. 'Well, you must remember that the Harlesden case was very peculiar. In fact, I think I may safely say that in some features it was unique—quite unique.'

'Quite so,' I replied, 'and that's exactly why it interests me, and why I want to know more about it. And I thought that if anybody could give me any information it would be you. What is your opinion of the matter?'

"It was a pretty downright sort of question, and my doctor looked rather taken aback.

" 'Well,' he said, 'as I fancy your motive in inquiring into the question must be mere curiosity, I think I may tell you my opinion with tolerable freedom. So, Mr. Dyson, if you want to know my theory, it is this: I believe that Dr. Black killed his wife.'

"'But the verdict,' I answered, 'the verdict was given from

your own evidence.'

"'Quite so; the verdict was given in accordance with the evidence of my colleague and myself, and, under the circumstances, I think the jury acted very sensibly. In fact, I don't see what else they could have done. But I stick to my opinion, mind you, and I say this also. I don't wonder at Black's doing what I firmly believe he did. I think he was justified.'

"'Justified! How could that be?' I asked. I was astonished, as you may imagine, at the answer I had got. The doctor wheeled round his chair and looked steadily at me for a moment before he answered.

" 'I suppose you are not a man of science yourself? No; then it would be of no use my going into detail. I have always been firmly opposed myself to any partnership between physiology and psychology. I believe that both are bound to suffer. No one recognizes more decidedly than I do the impassable gulf, the fathomless abyss that separates the world of consciousness from the sphere of matter. We know that every change of consciousness is accompanied by a rear-rangement of the molecules in the grey matter; and that is all. What the link between them is, or why they occur together, we do not know, and the most authorities believe that we never can know. Yet, I will tell you that as I did my work, the knife in my hand, I felt convinced, in spite of all theories, that what lay before me was not the brain of a dead woman—not the brain of a human being at all. Of course I saw the face; but it was quite placid, devoid of all expression. It must have been a beautiful face, no doubt, but I can honestly say that I would not have looked in that face when there was life behind it for a thousand guineas, no, nor for twice that sum.'." 'My dear sir,' I said, 'you surprise me extremely. You say that it was not the brain of a human being. What was it, then?'

"'The brain of a devil.' He spoke quite coolly, and never moved a muscle. 'The brain of a devil,' he repeated, 'and I have no

doubt that Black found some way of putting an end to it. I don't
blame him if he did. Whatever Mrs. Black was, she was not fit to
stay in this world. Will you have anything more? No? Good-night,
good-night.'

"It was a queer sort of opinion to get from a man of science, wasn't it? When he was saying that he would not have looked
on that face when alive for a thousand guineas, or two thousand
guineas, I was thinking of the face I had seen, but I said nothing. I
went again to Harlesden, and passed from one shop to another,
making small purchases, and trying to find out whether there was
anything about the Blacks which was not already common property, but there was very little to hear. One of the tradesmen to
whom I spoke said he had known the dead woman well; she used
to buy of him such quantities of grocery as were required for their
small household, for they never kept a servant, but had a char-
woman in occasionally, and she had not seen Mrs. Black for
months before she died. According to this man Mrs. Black was 'a
nice lady,' always kind and considerate, and so fond of her husband
and he of her, as every one thought. And yet, to put the doctor's
opinion on one side, I knew what I had seen. And then after thinking it over, and putting one thing with another, it seemed to me
that the only person likely to give me much assistance would be
Black himself, and I made up my mind to find him. Of course he
wasn't to be found in Harlesden; he had left, I was told, directly
after the funeral. Everything in the house had been sold, and one
fine day Black got into the train with a small portmanteau, and
went, nobody knew where. It was a chance if he were ever heard of
again, and it was by a mere chance that I came across him at last. I
was walking one day along Gray's Inn Road, not bound for anywhere in particular, but looking about me, as usual, and holding on
to my hat, for it was a gusty day in early March, and the wind was
making the treetops in the Inn rock and quiver. I had come up
from the Holborn end, and I had almost got to Theobald's Road

when I noticed a man walking in front of me, leaning on a stick, and to all appearance very feeble. There was something about his look that made me curious, I don't know why, and I began to walk briskly with the idea of overtaking him, when of a sudden his hat blew off and came bounding along the pavement to my feet. Of course I rescued the hat, and gave it a glance as I went towards its owner. It was a biography in itself; a Piccadilly maker's name in the inside, but t don't think a beggar would have picked it out of the gutter. Then I looked up and saw Dr. Black of Harlesden waiting for me. A queer thing, wasn't it? But, Salisbury, what a change! When I saw Dr. Black come down the steps of his house at Harlesden he was an upright man, walking firmly with well-built limbs; a man, should say, in the prime of his life. And now before me there crouched this wretched creature, bent and feeble, with shrunken cheeks, and hair that was whitening fast, and limbs that trembled and shook together, and misery in his eyes. He thanked me for bringing him his hat, saying, 'I don't think I should ever have got it, I can't run much now. A gusty day, sir, isn't it?' and with this he was turning way, but by little and little I contrived to draw him into the current of conversation, and we walked together eastward. I think the man would have been glad to get rid of me; but I didn't intend to let him go, and he stopped at last in front of a miserable house in a miserable street. It was, I verily believe, one of the most wretched quarters I have ever seen: houses that must have been sordid and hideous enough when new, that had gathered foulness with every year, and now seemed to lean and totter to their fall. 'I live up there,' said Black, pointing to the tiles, 'not in the front—in the back. I am very quiet there. I won't ask you to come in now, but perhaps some other day—' I caught him up at that, and told him I should be only too glad to come and see him. He gave me an odd sort of glance, as if he were wondering what on earth I or anybody else could care about him, and I left him fumbling with his latchkey. I think you will say I did pretty well when I tell you that within a few weeks I had made myself an intimate friend of Black's. I shall never forget the first time I went to his room; I hope I shall never see such abject, squalid misery again. The foul paper, from which all pattern or trace of a pattern had long vanished, subdued and penetrated with the grime of the evil street, was hanging in mouldering pennons from the wall. Only at the end of the room was it possible to stand upright, and the sight of the wretched bed and the odour of corruption that pervaded the place made me turn faint and sick. Here I found him munching a piece of bread; he seemed surprised to find that I had kept my promise, but he gave me his chair and sat on the bed while we talked. I used to go to see him often, and we had long conversations together, but he never mentioned Harlesden or his wife. I fancy that he supposed me ignorant of the matter, or thought that if I had heard of it, I should never connect the respectable Dr. Black of Harlesden with a poor garreteer in the backwoods of London. He was a strange man, and as we sat together smoking, I often wondered whether he were made or sane, for I think the wildest dreams of Paracelsus and the Rosicrucians would appear plain and sober fact compared with the theories I have heard him earnestly advance in that grimy den of his. I once ventured to hint something of the sort to him. I suggested that something he had said was in flat contradiction to all science and all experience.

'No,' he answered, 'not all experience, for mine counts for something. I am no dealer in unproved theories; what I say I have proved for myself, and at a terrible cost. There is a region of knowledge which you will never know, which wise men seeing from afar off shun like the plague, as well they may, but into that region I have gone. If you knew, if you could even dream of what may be done, of what one or two men have done in this quiet world of ours, your very soul would shudder and faint within you. What you have heard from me has been but the merest husk and outer covering of true science—that science which means death, and that which is more

153

awful than death, to those who gain it. No, when men say that there are strange things in the world, they little know the awe and the terror that dwell always with them and about them.'

There was a sort of fascination about the man that drew me to him, and I was quite sorry to have to leave London for a month or two; I missed his odd talk. A few days after I came back to town I thought I would look him up, but when I gave the two rings at the bell that used to summon him, there was no answer. I rang and rang again, and was just turning to go away, when the door opened and a dirty woman asked me what I wanted. From her look I fancy she took me for a plain-clothes officer after one of her lodgers, but when I inquired if Mr. Black were in, she gave me a stare of another kind. 'There's no Mr. Black lives here,' she said. 'He's gone. He's dead these six weeks.' I always thought he was a bit queer in his head, or else had been and got into some trouble or other. He used to go out every morning from ten till one, and one Monday morning we heard him come in, and go into his room and shut the door, and a few minutes after, just as we was a-sitting down to our dinner, there was such a scream that I thought I should have gone right off. And then we heard a stamping, and down he came, raging and cursing most dreadful, swearing he had been robbed of something that was worth millions. And then he just dropped down in the passage, and we thought he was dead. We got him up to his room, and put him on his bed, and I just sat there and waited, while my 'usband he went for the doctor. And there was the winder wide open, and a little tin box he had lying on the floor open and empty, but of course nobody could possibly have got in at the winder, and as for him having anything that was worth anything, it's nonsense, for he was often weeks and weeks behind with his rent, and my 'usband he threatened often and often to turn him into the street, for, as he said, we've got a living to make like other people—and, of course, that's true; but, somehow, I didn't like to do it, though he was an odd kind of a man, and I fancy had been better off. And then the doctor came and looked at him, and said as he couldn't do nothing, and that night he died as I was a-sitting by his bed; and I can tell you that, with one thing and another, we lost money by him, for the few bits of clothes as he had were worth next to nothing when they came to be sold.' I gave the woman half a sovereign for her trouble, and went home thinking of Dr. Black and the epitaph she had made him, and wondering at his strange fancy that he had been robbed. I take it that he had very little to fear on that score, poor fellow; but I suppose that he was really mad, and died in a sudden access of his mania. His landlady said that once or twice when she had had occasion to go into his room (to dun the poor wretch for his rent, most likely), he would keep her at the door for about a min-ute, and that when she came in she would find him putting away his tin box in the corner by the window; I suppose he had be-come possessed with the idea of some great treasure, and fancied himself a wealthy man in the midst of all his misery. Explicit, my tale is ended, and you see that though I knew Black, I knew noth-ing of his wife or of the history of her death— That's the Harlesden case, Salisbury, and I think it interests me all the more deeply because there does not seem the shadow of a possibility that I or anyone else will ever know more about it.

What do you think of it?"

"Well, Dyson, I must say that I think you have contrived to surround the whole thing with a mystery of your own making. I go for the doctor's solution: Black murdered his wife, being himself in all probability an undeveloped lunatic."

"What? Do you believe, then, that this woman was some-thing too awful, too terrible to be allowed to remain on the earth? You will remember that the doctor said it was the brain of a devil?"

"Yes, yes, but he was speaking, of course, metaphorically. It's really quite a simple matter if you only look at it like that."

"Ah, well, you may be right; but yet I am sure you are not. Well, well, it's not good discussing it any more. A little more Benedictine? That's right; try some of this tobacco. Didn't you say that you had been bothered by something—something which happened that night we dined together?"

"Yes, I have been worried, Dyson, worried a great deal. I— But it's such a trivial matter— indeed, such an absurdity—that I feel ashamed to trouble you with it."

"Never mind, let's have it, absurd or not."

With many hesitations, and with much inward resentment of the folly of the thing, Salisbury told his tale, and repeated reluctantly the absurd intelligence and the absurder doggerel of the scrap of paper, expecting to hear Dyson burst out into a roar of laughter.

"Isn't it too bad that I should let myself be bothered by such stuff as that?" he asked, when he had stuttered out the jingle of once, and twice, and thrice.

Dyson had listened to it all gravely, even to the end, and meditated for a few minutes in silence.

"Yes," he said at length, "it was a curious chance, your taking shelter in that archway just as those two went by. But I don't know that I should call what was written on the paper nonsense; it is bizarre certainly but I expect it has a meaning for somebody. Just repeat it again, will you, and I will write it down. Perhaps we might find a cipher of some sort, though I hardly think we shall."

Again had the reluctant lips of Salisbury slowly to stammer out the rubbish that he abhorred, while Dyson jotted it down on a slip of paper."Look over it, will you?" he said, when it was done; "it may be important that I should have every word in its place. Is that all right?"

"Yes; that is an accurate copy. But I don't think you will get much out of it. Depend upon it, it is mere nonsense, a wanton scribble. I must be going now, Dyson. No, no more; that stuff of yours is pretty strong. Good-night."

"I suppose you would like to hear from me, if I did find out anything?"

"No, not I; I don't want to hear about the thing again. You may regard the discovery, if it is one, as your own."

"Very well. Good-night."

# IV

A good many hours after Salisbury had returned to the company of the green rep chairs, Dyson still sat at his desk, itself a Japanese romance, smoking many pipes, and meditating over his friend's story. The bizarre quality of the inscription which had annoyed Salisbury was to him an attraction, and now and again he took it up and scanned thoughtfully what he had written, especially the quaint jingle at the end. It was a token, a symbol, he decided, and not a cipher, and the woman who had flung it away was in all probability entirely ignorant of its meaning; she was but the agent of the "Sam" she had abused and discarded, and he too was again the agent of someone unknown; possibly of the individual styled Q, who had been forced to visit his French friends. But what to make of "Traverse Handel S." Here was the root and source of the enigma, and not all the tobacco of Virginia seemed likely to suggest any clue here. It seemed almost hopeless, but Dyson regarded himself as the Wellington of mysteries, and went to bed feeling assured that sooner or later he would hit upon the right track. For the next few days he was deeply engaged in his literary labours, labours which were a profound mystery even to the most intimate of his friends, who searched the railway bookstalls in vain for the result of so many hours spent at the Japanese bureau in company with strong tobacco and black tea. On this occasion Dyson confined himself to his room for four days, and it was with genuine relief that he laid down his pen and went out into the streets in quest of relaxation and fresh air. The gas-lamps were being lighted, and the fifth edition of the evening papers was being howled through the streets, and Dyson, feeling that he wanted quiet, turned away from the clamorous Strand, and began to trend away to the north-west. Soon he found himself in streets that echoed to his footsteps, and crossing a broad new thoroughfare, and verging still to the west, Dyson discovered that he had penetrated to the depths of Soho. Here again was life; rare vintages of France and Italy, at prices which seemed contemptibly small, allured the passer-by; here were cheeses, vast and rich, here olive oil, and here a grove of Rabelaisian sausages; while in a neighbouring shop the whole press of Paris appeared to be on sale. In the middle of the roadway a strange miscellany of nations sauntered to and fro, for there cab and hansom rarely ventured; and from window over window the inhabitants looked forth in pleased contemplation of the scene. Dyson made his way slowly along, mingling with the crowd on the cobble-stones, listening to the queer babel of French and German, and Italian and English, glancing now and again at the shop windows with their levelled batteries of bottles, and had almost gained the end of the street, when his attention was arrested by a small shop at the corner, a vivid contrast to its neighbours. It was the typical shop of the poor quarter; a shop entirely English. Here were vended tobacco and sweets, cheap pipes of clay and cherrywood; penny exercise books and penholders jostled for precedence with comic songs, and story papers with appalling cuts showed that romance claimed its place beside the actualities of the evening paper, the bills of which fluttered at the doorway.

Dyson glanced up at the name above the door, and stood by the kennel trembling, for a sharp pang, the pang of one who has made a discovery, had for a moment left him incapable of motion.

The name over the shop was Travers. Dyson looked up again, this time at the corner of the wall above the lamppost, and read in white letters on a blue ground the words "Handel Street, W. C." and the legend was repeated in fainter letters just below. He gave a little sigh of satisfaction, and without more ado walked boldly into the shop, and stared full in the face of the fat man who was sitting behind the counter. The fellow rose to his feet, and returned the stare a little curiously, and then began in stereotyped phrase— "What can I do for you, sir?"

Dyson enjoyed the situation and a dawning perplexity on the man's face. He propped his stick carefully against the counter and leaning over it, said slowly and impressively— "Once around the grass, and twice around the lass, and thrice around the maple-tree."

Dyson had calculated on his words producing an effect, and he was not disappointed. The vendor of the miscellanies gasped, open-mouthed like a fish, and steadied himself against the counter. When he spoke, after a short interval, it was in a hoarse mutter, tremulous and unsteady.

"Would you mind saying that again, sir? I didn't quite catch it."

"My good man, I shall most certainly do nothing of the kind. You heard what I said perfectly well. You have got a clock in your shop, I see; an admirable timekeeper, I have no doubt. Well, I give you a minute by your own clock."

The man looked about him in a perplexed indecision, and Dyson felt that it was time to be bold.

"Look here, Travers, the time is nearly up. You have heard of Q, I think. Remember, I hold your life in my hands. Now!"

Dyson was shocked at the result of his own audacity. The man shrank and shrivelled in terror, the sweat poured down a face of ashy white, and he held up his hands before him.

"Mr. Davies, Mr. Davies, don't say that—don't for Heaven's sake. I didn't know you at first, I didn't indeed. Good God! Mr. Davies, you wouldn't ruin me? I'll get it in a moment."

"You had better not lose any more time."

The man slunk piteously out of his own shop, and went

into a back parlour. Dyson heard his trembling fingers fumbling with a bunch of keys, and the creak of an opening box. He came back presently with a small package neatly tied up in brown paper in his hands, and still, full of terror, handed it to Dyson.

"I'm glad to be rid of it," he said. "I'll take no more jobs of this sort."

Dyson took the parcel and his stick, and walked out of the shop with a nod, turning round as he passed the door. Travers had sunk into his seat, his face still white with terror, with one hand over his eyes, and Dyson speculated a good deal as he walked rapidly away as to what queer chords those could be on which he had played so roughly. He hailed the first hansom he could see and drove home, and when he had lit his hanging lamp, and laid his parcel on the table, he paused for a moment, wondering on what strange thing the lamp-light would soon shine. He locked his door, and cut the strings, and unfolded the paper layer after layer, and came at last to a small wooden box, simply but solidly made. There was no lock, and Dyson had simply to raise the lid, and as he did so he drew a long breath and started back. The lamp seemed to glimmer feebly like a single candle, but the whole room blazed with light—and not with light alone, but with a thousand colours, with all the glories of some painted window; and upon the walls of his room and on the familiar furniture, the glow flamed back and seemed to flow again to its source, the little wooden box. For there upon a bed of soft wool lay the most splendid jewel, a jewel such as Dyson had never dreamed of, and within it shone the blue of far skies, and the green of the sea by the shore, and the red of the ruby, and deep violet rays, and in the middle of all it seemed aflame as if a fountain of fire rose up, and fell, and rose again with sparks like stars for drops.

Dyson gave a long deep sigh, and dropped into his chair, and put his hands over his eyes to think.

The jewel was like an opal, but from a long experience of

the shop windows he knew there was no such thing as an opal one quarter or one eighth of its size. He looked at the stone again, with a feeling that was almost awe, and placed it gently on the table under the lamp, and watched the wonderful flame that shone and sparkled in its centre, and then turned to the box, curious to know whether it might contain other marvels. He lifted the bed of wool on which the opal had reclined, and saw beneath, no more jewels, but a little old pocketbook, worn and shabby with use. Dyson opened it at the first leaf, and dropped the book again appalled. He had read the name of the owner, neatly written in blue ink: Steven Black, M.D., Oranmore, Devon Road, Harlesden.

It was several minutes before Dyson could bring himself to open the book a second time; he remembered the wretched exile in his garret; and his strange talk, and the memory too of the face he had seen at the window, and of what the specialist had said, surged up in his mind, and as he held his finger on the cover, he shivered, dreading what might be written within. When at last he held it in his hand, and turned the pages, he found that the first two leaves were blank, but the third was covered with clear, minute writing, and Dyson began to read with the light of the opal flaming in his eyes.

# V

"Ever since I was a young man"—the record began—"I devoted all my leisure and a good deal of time that ought to have been given to other studies to the investigation of curious and obscure branches of knowledge. What are commonly called the pleasures of life had never any attractions for me, and I lived alone in London, avoiding my fellow students, and in my turn avoided by them as a man self-absorbed and unsympathetic. So long as I could gratify my desire of knowledge of a peculiar kind, knowledge of which the very existence is a profound secret to most men, I was intensely happy, and I have often spent whole nights sitting in the darkness of my room, and thinking of the strange world on the brink of which I trod. My professional studies, however, and the necessity of obtaining a degree, for some time forced my more obscure employment into the background, and soon after I had qualified I met Agnes, who became my wife. We took a new house in this remote suburb, and I began the regular routine of a sober practice, and for some months lived happily enough, sharing in the life about me, and only thinking at odd intervals of that occult science which had once fascinated my whole being. I had learnt enough of the paths I had begun to tread to know that they were beyond all expression difficult and dangerous, that to persevere meant in all probability the wreck of a life, and that they led to regions so terrible, that the mind of man shrinks appalled at the very thought.

Moreover, the quiet and the peace I had enjoyed since my marriage had wiled me away to a great extent from places where I knew no peace could dwell. But suddenly—I think indeed it was the work of a single night, as I lay awake on my bed gazing into the darkness—suddenly, I say, the old desire, the former longing, returned, and returned with a force that had been intensified ten times by its absence; and when the day dawned and I looked out of the window, and saw with haggard eyes the sunrise in the east, I knew that my doom had been pronounced; that as I had gone far, so now I must go farther with unfaltering steps. I turned to the bed where my wife was sleeping peacefully, and lay down again, weeping bitter tears, for the sun had set on our happy life and had risen with a dawn of terror to us both. I will not set down here in minute detail what followed; outwardly I went about the day's labour as before, saying nothing to my wife. But she soon saw that I had changed; I spent my spare time in a room which I had fitted up as a laboratory, and often I crept upstairs in the grey dawn of the morning, when the light of many lamps still glowed over London; and each night I had stolen a step nearer to that great abyss which I was to bridge over, the gulf between the world of consciousness and the world of matter.

My experiments were many and complicated in their nature, and it was some months before I realized whither they all pointed, and when this was borne in upon me in a moment's time, I felt my face whiten and my heart still within me. But the power to draw back, the power to stand before the doors that now opened wide before me and not to enter in, had long ago been absent; the way was closed, and I could only pass onward. My position was as utterly hopeless as that of the prisoner in an utter dungeon, whose only light is that of the dungeon above him; the doors were shut and escape was impossible. Experiment after experiment gave the same result, and I knew, and shrank even as the thought passed through my mind, that in the work I had to do there must be elements which no laboratory could furnish, which no scales could ever measure. In that work, from which even I doubted to escape with life, life itself must enter; from some human being there must be drawn that essence which men call the soul, and in its place (for in the scheme of the world there is no vacant chamber)—in its place would enter in what the lips can hardly utter, what the mind cannot conceive without a horror more awful than the horror of death itself. And when I knew this, I knew also on whom this fate would fall; I looked into my wife's eyes. Even at that hour, if I had gone out and taken a rope and hanged myself, I might have escaped, and she also, but in no other way. At last I told her all. She shuddered, and wept, and called on her dead mother for help, and asked me if I had no mercy, and I could only sigh. I concealed nothing from her; I told her what she would become, and what would enter in where her life had been; I told her of all the shame and of all the horror. You who will read this when I am dead—if indeed I allow this record to survive—you who have opened the box and have seen what lies there, if you could understand what lies hidden in that opal! For one night my wife consented to what I asked of her, consented with the tears running down her beautiful face, and hot shame flushing red over her neck and breast, consented to undergo this for me. I threw open the window, and we looked together at the sky and the dark earth for the last time; it was a fine star-light night, and there was a pleasant breeze blowing: and I kissed her on her lips, and her tears ran down upon my face. That night she came down to my laboratory, and there, with shutters bolted and barred down, with curtains drawn thick and close, so that the very stars might be shut out from the sight of that room, while the crucible hissed and boiled over the lamp, I did what had to be done, and led out what was no longer a woman. But on the table the opal flamed and sparkled with such light as no eyes of man have ever gazed on, and the rays of the flame that was within it flashed and glittered, and shone even to my heart. My wife had only asked one thing of me; that when there came at last what I had told her, I would kill her. I have kept that promise.".There was nothing more. Dyson let the little pocketbook fall, and turned and looked again at the opal with its flaming inmost light, and then with unutterable irresistible horror surging up in his heart, grasped the jewel, and flung it on the ground, and trampled it beneath his heel. His face was white with terror as he turned away, and for a moment stood sick and trembling, and then with a start he leapt across the room and steadied himself against the door. There was an angry hiss, as of steam escaping under great pressure, and as he gazed, motionless, a volume of heavy yellow smoke was slowly issuing from the very centre of the jewel, and wreathing itself in snakelike coils above it. And then a thin white flame burst forth from the smoke, and shot up into the air and vanished; and on the ground there lay a thing like a cinder, black and crumbling to the touch.

THE END

*Also from Benediction Books …*
**Wandering Between Two Worlds: Essays on Faith and Art**
**Anita Mathias**
Benediction Books, 2007
152 pages
ISBN: 0955373700

Available from www.amazon.com, www.amazon.co.uk

In these wide-ranging lyrical essays, Anita Mathias writes, in lush, lovely prose, of her naughty Catholic childhood in Jamshedpur, India; her large, eccentric family in Mangalore, a sea-coast town converted by the Portuguese in the sixteenth century; her rebellion and atheism as a teenager in her Himalayan boarding school, run by German missionary nuns, St. Mary's Convent, Nainital; and her abrupt religious conversion after which she entered Mother Teresa's convent in Calcutta as a novice. Later rich, elegant essays explore the dualities of her life as a writer, mother, and Christian in the United States-- Domesticity and Art, Writing and Prayer, and the experience of being "an alien and stranger" as an immigrant in America, sensing the need for roots.

## About the Author

Anita Mathias is the author of *Wandering Between Two Worlds: Essays on Faith and Art*. She has a B.A. and M.A. in English from Somerville College, Oxford University, and an M.A. in Creative Writing from the Ohio State University, USA. Anita won a National Endowment of the Arts fellowship in Creative Nonfiction in 1997. She lives in Oxford, England with her husband, Roy, and her daughters, Zoe and Irene.

Anita's website:
    http://www.anitamathias.com, and
Anita's blog Dreaming Beneath the Spires:
    http://dreamingbeneaththespires.blogspot.com

**The Church That Had Too Much**
**Anita Mathias**
Benediction Books, 2010
52 pages
ISBN: 9781849026567

Available from www.amazon.com, www.amazon.co.uk

The Church That Had Too Much was very well-intentioned. She
wanted to love God, she wanted to love people, but she was both
hampered by her muchness and the abundance of her possessions,
and beset by ambition, power struggles and snobbery. Read about
the surprising way The Church That Had Too Much began to re-
solve her problems in this deceptively simple and enchanting fable.

## About the Author

Anita Mathias is the author of *Wandering Between Two Worlds: Essays
on Faith and Art*. She has a B.A. and M.A. in English from Somerville College, Oxford University, and an M.A. in Creative Writing
from the Ohio State University, USA. Anita won a National Endowment of the Arts fellowship in Creative Nonfiction in 1997.
She lives in Oxford, England with her husband, Roy, and her
daughters, Zoe and Irene.

Anita's website:
  http://www.anitamathias.com, and
Anita's blog Dreaming Beneath the Spires:
  http://dreamingbeneaththespires.blogspot.com